299

P9-CQA-523

Addie McCormick

AND THE MYSTERY OF THE SKELETON KEY

Leanne Lucas

HARVEST HOUSE PUBLISHERS
Eugene, Oregon 97402

**Addie McCormick and the Mystery
of the Skeleton Key**

Copyright © 1993 by Leanne Lucas
Published by Harvest House Publishers
Eugene, Oregon 97402

Library of Congress Cataloging-in-Publication Data

Lucas, Leanne, 1955–
    Addie McCormick and the mystery of the skeleton key/
Leanne Lucas.
        p.   cm. — (Addie adventure book ; 5)
    Summary: When relatives gather to celebrate her grand-
mother's birthday, Addie and her cousin are determined
to find the family treasure supposedly left by Addie's
namesake.
    ISBN 1-56507-147-6
    [1. Family life—Fiction.   2. Mystery and detective sto-
ries. 3. Christian life—Fiction.] I. Title. II. Series: Lucas,
Leanne, 1955– Addie adventure book ; 5.
PZ7.L96963Adc   1993   93-806
[Fic]—dc20   CIP
                                                              AC

Printed in the United States of America.

For my husband, David,
who helps me think
and makes me laugh.

November 9, 1860

Winnie dear,

What a joy it was to spend time with you and your daughter this past spring. How time flies! Already winter is upon us, and I'm sure my precious namesake grows more lovely each day.

Given the scope of events that have occurred in our country in the last week, I felt it only proper to add this gift to your collection of treasures for young Addie. I believe this, more than all else, will prove to be a treasure of great worth for her.

I do not think, however, that this is a portent of Addie's future. My prayer is that she will grow up not in the shadow of great men, but following in their footsteps.

God keep you in His care.

All my love,
Addie N.

Winnie Johnson married Harrison Haile in 1858 WJH
| Daughter Adlon born in 1859

Adlon Haile married Randolph Kelley in 1876 AHK
| Daughter Nolda born in 1877

Nolda Kelley married Samuel Elder in 1895 NKE
| Daughter Adlon born in 1897

Adlon Elder married Theodore Powell in 1915 AEP
| Daughter Londa born in 1916

Londa Powell married Edward Francis in 1934 LPF
| Daughter Adlon born in 1935

Adlon Francis married Kenneth McCormick in 1953 AFM
| Son Donal born in 1955

Donal John McCormick married Gwen Thompson in 1977
| Daughter Adlon born in 1981

Adlon Jane McCormick

CHAPTER 1

The Legacy

Addie McCormick shifted restlessly in her chair. She tried to listen as Mrs. Himmel's voice droned on about the Civil War. Her gaze wandered to the window and she sighed.

The trees in the school yard were still bare, the grass was still brown, and the glaring brightness of the afternoon sun belied the fact that it was only 29 degrees out. Winter in Illinois could be bitter, even in early March. Her father said they hadn't seen the last of the snow. Addie hoped he was wrong. Their trip to Gram's might be canceled if—

The trip! Addie couldn't keep her mind off the mini-vacation her parents had planned for the next few days. Addie was going to miss three days of school so they could travel to Wisconsin to celebrate Gram's sixtieth birthday. All her uncles and aunts and cousins would be there. She couldn't wait to see her "twin" cousin Jake, and her newest cousin, Lindsey, and—

"Would you agree with that answer, Addie?" The sound of Mrs. Himmel's quiet voice derailed the train of thought that was carrying Addie to Wisconsin, and she came back to her sixth-grade classroom with a jolt. All her classmates were turned in their seats watching her, waiting for her answer.

Addie gave Nick Brady, her best friend, a quick glance and he mouthed the word "no" with a slight shake of his head.

"No, I don't agree," she said slowly.

"You don't sound very sure of yourself, Addie. Why not?" Mrs. Himmel had an amused look on her face.

Addie gave up the deception. She had never been good at lying. "Because I don't trust Nick," she declared, and the rest of the class burst into laughter. Nick turned bright red, but he grinned.

Mrs. Himmel tried not to smile and failed. "That's wise," she said. "He was setting you up. I think we'd all agree, Abraham Lincoln *was* the sixteenth president of the United States."

Addie was so embarrassed she covered her eyes with one hand and slid low in her chair. Over the laughter she heard Mrs. Himmel say, "I'll overlook your daydreaming this time, Addie. I'm sure your memory of U.S. history will improve once you come back from Wisconsin."

The final bell rang, and the laughter was replaced by desk lids slamming open and closed again and chairs scraping across the floor. The children filled their backpacks with the night's homework and took turns getting coats and hats and gloves from the rack on the back wall. The country kids lined up at the door first.

Nick hung back and stopped at Addie's desk. She tried to glare at her friend, but his ornery grin was catching.

"I'll get you back, Nick," she threatened good-naturedly.

"I don't care," he laughed. "It was worth it!"

"Nick," Mrs. Himmel called over the noise. "Buses are leaving."

Nick ran for the door, but he called over his shoulder, "Bring me something from Wisconsin, Addie. Somethin' expensive!"

"You wish!" Addie shot back, but they both knew she would, even if it wasn't expensive.

Addie watched from the window as the buses filled to capacity with noisy, red-cheeked kids. Normally, she'd be on one of those buses. She and Nick were neighbors. They had both moved to the area the summer before. Their houses were located in the middle of acres of farmland. Their friendship had originated out of necessity—no other children lived close by—and developed out of compatibility. They both had great imaginations. What one didn't think of, the other did.

Addie's parents pulled into the school parking lot. She grabbed her backpack and ran past the line of city kids waiting to be dismissed.

"See ya, Addie!" Hillary Jackson called after her. Hillary was a good friend from her church. Addie waved as a chorus of goodbyes followed her out the door and she heard Andy Meeker grumble, "How'd she luck out of school for the next three days, anyway?"

Addie jumped in the backseat and beamed at her parents. "Let's go!" she exclaimed.

Her father grinned but held up his hand. "First things first," he said. "Got all your homework?"

"Yes. I went over the list twice today with Mrs. Himmel."

"Are you sure you packed everything you wanted to take before you left for school this morning?" her mother asked.

"Yes." Addie nodded again. "I went through my suitcase four times last night and twice this morning."

"Did you give the hermit crabs extra food?"

"Yes."

"Unplug your curling iron?"

"Yes!" Addie was getting impatient.

"Fill the tank and check the oil?"

"*Dad!*"

"Oh, sorry. That was my job wasn't it?" He grinned at Mrs. McCormick and Addie kicked the back of his seat lightly. She loved her dad but sometimes his sense of humor drove her crazy.

"I guess we're ready then," he said. "Why don't we pray?"

Addie leaned back and closed her eyes while her dad prayed for their safety on the trip to Wisconsin. He asked the Lord to bless the time they spent with his family and prayed a special blessing for Gram.

When Addie opened her eyes she gave a startled squeal. Hillary and Andy had their faces plastered to her window with their mouths wide open. Addie began to giggle and Mr. McCormick rolled down his window.

"You're lucky this car is warmed up or your lips would be on their way to Wisconsin!" he grinned. Andy and Hillary waved as the McCormicks left the school and Addie sat back with a contented smile.

The drive to Wisconsin took five hours and the time seemed to drag. Addie read for the first hour or so, but soon the sun set. After a brief stop for supper, they were on the road again, and Addie listened to Carman on her portable tape player. After two bathroom breaks, they were only an hour from Gram's house. Addie tried to stay awake, but the long drive and the steady hum of the engine soon lulled her to sleep. The next thing she knew, her mother was tapping her knee.

"We're in Camp Point, Addie. Wake up."

Addie sat up with a start. Had she missed the houses? No. She relaxed and peered out the window.

Camp Point was a middle-sized town, very old, and filled with "old money," as her mom said. Many of the houses that lined the streets were exquisite and Addie loved to look at them, especially at night. If you were lucky, their curtains were open and you could catch a glimpse of long, winding staircases or stately old fireplaces with big oak mantels and crystal chandeliers reflected in the mirrors above them. Her father drove slowly and Addie peered into every lighted window.

The steep hill that bordered the north end of Camp Point had few houses on its lone street, Butternut Lane. Gram's was the last, at the very top of the hill. It was a beautiful old house, one of the nicest in town. Addie was glad she didn't have to stare into it through open curtains on her way by in a car.

The house was dark except for the light Gram always left on by the carriage house in back. Her father pulled down the drive toward the light, and as if by magic, the automatic door on the carriage house opened silently. All three McCormicks cheered.

"I can't believe it!" Addie exclaimed. "We actually beat Uncle Denny this time!"

Whenever the family gathered at Gram's, the first to arrive got the privilege of parking their car in the carriage house next to Gram's Lincoln. More often than not, Uncle Denny—the only bachelor in the family—arrived first. Everyone else had to pull around the carriage house and park in back.

"She must have been watching for us," Mr. McCormick said. He steered the car through the door and it slid shut behind them. Addie was out of the backseat before the car was turned off. Gram was coming down the enclosed walkway that connected the carriage house to the main house and Addie ran to meet her. She threw herself into the older woman's arms and Gram laughed at her enthusiasm.

"Oh, Addie, another year and you won't be able to do that. You'll knock me right off my feet. Look at you!"

Gram held her at arms' length and studied her with pride, then pulled her close for another hug. "Come on, let's get inside. I've got water on for hot chocolate."

Addie's father had opened the trunk to get the suitcases. Now he called down the chilly corridor, "That's okay, Mom, don't worry about me. I'm only the chauffeur. I'll just drop off Addie's luggage and be on my way."

"You'll get your hug inside, where it's warm. Hurry up!" The senior Mrs. McCormick gave Addie a wink and opened the door to the spacious kitchen.

Gram had changed the color scheme again—now everything was peach—but the basics were the same: lots of oak cabinets with wide oak trim around all the doors and a knotty pine floor that gleamed with fresh polish. The walls were lined with pictures of the family, especially Addie's Grandpa. There were letters he had written home during World War II, as well as things like ration coupons for bread and sugar and gas. Addie never tired of looking at Gram's walls. She always discovered something she hadn't noticed before.

Addie's mom and dad came in and got their hugs. Mr. McCormick dropped the suitcases in the hall and Gram pulled out cups and saucers for everyone, talking a mile a minute while she worked.

Addie took the time to study Gram carefully. Had she changed in the last six months? After all, she *was* 60 now, or almost. Grandpa had died last year at 66. Addie didn't think she could bear to lose both of them.

Gram was a thin woman and tall, almost five foot, ten inches. She carried her height well. Her once black hair was now a beautiful silver, cut stylishly short, and her clear blue eyes sparkled behind glasses that slipped down her nose every now and then. She moved easily as she worked, filling cups and pulling spoons out of a drawer under the counter.

Addie smiled to herself, satisfied that Gram was still Gram. The older woman caught her smile and plopped two fat marshmallows into Addie's cup before she finally sat down.

"I'm so glad you're the first ones to arrive. I wanted to have Addie to myself when I gave her her legacy."

Addie's sip of hot chocolate turned into a gulp and she began to cough. "My what?" she managed to choke out.

Gram looked at her son in surprise. "Didn't you tell her?"

Mr. McCormick grinned sheepishly. "It's a five-hour drive up here," he said when Addie could breathe again. "That's long enough as it is. If you were wondering about a 'legacy' all the way here it would have seemed twice as long."

Gram took her hand. "I guess I get all the honors then. That's even better." She took a deep breath and squeezed Addie's hand. Addie tried to stop the shiver of anticipation that went up her spine.

"Of course you know that you were given my name when you were born. Adlon, or some variation of that name, has been given to a child in every generation of our family since the Civil War." She paused, and Addie held her breath. "Did you ever wonder how that originated?"

Addie shrugged and shook her head.

Gram laughed. "Neither did I, to tell you the truth," she said in a conspiratorial whisper. "At least, not until my grandmother gave me this." She opened a cabinet above her and took out a small wooden box with the initial *A* carved on the top.

"This box belonged to the first 'Addie' in our family, your great-great-great-great-grandmother." Gram counted the greats on one hand to make sure she got the number correct. "It's been handed down through the generations, from one 'Addie' to the next. Now I'm giving it to you. I thought my sixtieth birthday was an appropriate time to pass on the legacy."

Addie didn't know what to say and she swallowed hard.

"Open it, honey," her father said.

Addie reached out with a trembling hand. The box opened easily. It was lined with plush red velvet that had worn thin on the bottom and around the edges.

The contents were simple. On top was a letter, yellow with age. It was torn at the creases that had been folded many times in the past one hundred and thirty-some years. The writing was faded and barely legible.

Beneath that was a key and Addie recognized it as a skeleton key. Miss Tisdale, their neighbor back home, had a skeleton key that could unlock the door to every room in her house.

Addie set the key down and went back to the letter. She took great care as she unfolded the dry yellow paper. The writing had faded so much it strained her eyes to read it. She concentrated in silence for several seconds.

"Addie! Read it," her father commanded with a frustrated laugh.

Addie frowned and shook her head. "I'll try," she said.

"'Winnie dear, What a . . . joy it was to spend time with you and your daughter . . . this past spring.' What a joy it was to spend time with you and your daughter this past spring," Addie repeated. "'How time flies! Already winter is upon us, and I'm sure my . . . my . . . precious namesake grows more lovely each day.

"'Given the scope of events that have occurred in our country in the last week, I felt it only proper to add this gift to your collection of treasures for young Addie. I believe this, more than all else, will prove to be a treasure of great worth for her.

"'I do not think, however, that this is a . . . portent of Addie's future. My prayer is that she will grow up not in the shadow of great men, but following in their footsteps.

"'God keep you in His care. All my love, Addie W.'

"Is this the key to the treasure?" Addie asked as she looked up from the letter.

Gram nodded. "I think so."

"Where is it?"

Gram smiled ruefully. "No one knows."

CHAPTER 2

The Fall

A letter, a skeleton key, and a lost treasure! It was all too much to take in and Addie could only stare at her grandmother, speechless. Gram laughed.

"Let me start at the beginning," she said. "I'll tell you everything I know, but I'm afraid it's not much."

"This letter," she tapped the yellowed paper gently, "talks about a gift from the original Addie to her namesake. Evidently, the original Addie and Winnie, your great-great-great-great-*great*-grandmother, were good friends."

"Probably great friends," Addie's dad murmured.

Gram rolled her eyes at the bad joke and ignored him. "Are you following me?"

Addie nodded. "I think so. The original Addie wasn't our relative. She was a good friend of my," Addie contemplated all the greats and said simply, "Gram plus five."

Her father chuckled and Gram smiled.

"Gram plus five named her baby Addie, after her friend," Addie continued. "Right?"

"Right," Gram said. "And that Addie passed the name on by naming *her* baby Nolda."

"Nolda?" Addie wrinkled her nose.

Gram nodded. "Adlon spelled backwards. Londa was another variation, and Donal was my idea. It's Irish. You know that, of course."

Mr. McCormick's full name was Donal John Mc-Cormick, but he went by John. Gram had given her firstborn son the name in case she never had a daughter. She never did, so the family name was passed on through Addie's father.

Gram frowned in concentration. "Actually, I think the name Adlon skipped generations. Let me see if I have this right. Gram plus four was named Adlon. Gram plus three was named Nolda. Gram plus two was another Adlon. Gram plus one was my mother, Londa. I'm another Adlon, your father was Donal . . . and now you."

"What year was the first Addie born?"

Gram closed her eyes and tapped her forehead gently with her index finger. She always did that when she was trying to remember something. "Before the Civil War. 1858 or 1859, I'm not sure. I have a family tree written up. It's in the attic in a box somewhere."

Addie rolled the heavy key around in the palm of her hand. "Did you ever try to find what the key fits?" she asked.

"Not really," Gram answered. "When my grandmother gave *me* the box, I was a young mother, busy with four boys under the age of six. It didn't mean much to me at the time. I know that disappointed her. It was years before I had the time to trace our name back to your gram plus four.

"I was able to get everyone's married names and birthdates," Gram continued, "plus bits and pieces of information about our family. But most of the relatives who might have known about the key have passed on."

Gram smiled at her grandaughter. "That's why I decided to give you the letter and key now, while you're still young. I don't have the energy to do any more digging myself, but I'll be glad to help you."

Addie felt a glow of excitement, but she hesitated. "What could I find that you didn't?" she asked her grandmother.

"Like I said, everyone I talked to had some scrap of information to tell me. I wrote everything down and put it all in a small box with the copy of our family tree. I'm sure there's something I missed that might help you out. Are you interested?"

"Nah," Addie's father answered for her. "These things bore Addie. She'd rather tube out, wouldn't you, kiddo?"

Addie threw a marshmallow at her father and he caught it easily, popping the whole thing in his mouth. She turned to Gram, her eyes sparkling. "I'd love it!"

"Good," Gram laughed. "First thing tomorrow morning we'll go to the attic and look for the box with all the information in it. All the photo albums are up there as well, even a couple of diaries my mother saved—"

She stopped at the look on Addie's face. "What's the matter, dear?"

The sparkle had faded from Addie's eyes. "Tomorrow?"

Addie's mom laughed. "Sweetheart, it's almost ten o'clock. Too late to start searching the attic."

Gram's expression softened at the disappointment on Addie's face. "Honey, if I knew where the box was, I'd go right this minute and get it. But I don't."

"What if I go upstairs with her?" Addie's father offered. "We'll just poke around for a few minutes," he assured Addie's mother. "Besides, we're on vacation. Who cares if she sleeps in tomorrow morning?"

Mrs. McCormick laughed and gave up without a fight.

"Thanks, Dad. I'll race you!"

Mr. McCormick jumped off the kitchen stool, but Addie beat him to the stairs and took them two at a time to the second floor. She turned and flew up the short flight of stairs to the third floor. She burst into the attic a step ahead of her father and dropped to the sofa that was against the wall just inside the door. A puff of dust wafted up around her. She reached over her head to flick on the light switch.

Mr. McCormick sat down heavily beside her. "I'm too old for this," he said between breaths. They both rested for a short time, then Addie stood up.

"Where do we start?" she asked.

Her father laughed and gestured around him. Addie made a face.

Gram was a pack rat. There were boxes everywhere, as well as racks of clothes, furniture covered with dusty white sheets, parts to machines that Addie didn't recognize, bushel baskets filled with canning jars, lamps without lamp shades, a box spring and mattress, an easel with a full palette of dried-up paints—the list went on and on.

"Let's start on this side and work our way around," her father suggested. He pulled the top off the box closest to the sofa and frowned.

"What is it?" Addie asked.

"Little glass jars," he said in a puzzled voice.

"You know Gram," Addie said. *"You never know when you'll need one of those."* She mimicked her grandmother's voice affectionately. "What's in that one?"

Mr. McCormick pulled the lid off the next box. "More boxes!"

"I've got just the box to wrap that in," they both said and burst into laughter.

"What are you guys up to?" said a gruff voice from the doorway and Addie gave a cry of delight.

"Uncle Denny!" She ran to give her youngest uncle a bear hug and he kissed the top of her head lightly. "We beat you!"

"Don't rub it in, Peepunk," he said. "Peepunk" was his pet name for Addie. "I had a flat tire or you wouldn't have."

John McCormick embraced his youngest brother. "Good to see you, Denny. How's life treating you?"

Denny grinned. "Come downstairs and I'll tell you all about it."

John glanced at his daughter. "I promised Addie—"

"Go ahead, Dad," Addie said. "I think I see what Gram means. She needs to come up in the morning and find that box. I'll just look around a little and be right down, okay?"

"Okay, kiddo." He winked and gave her cheek a light pat. "Don't be long." Their voices faded quickly down the attic stairs, and Addie was left alone.

She decided to skip the great big boxes. *Gram said she put everything in a small box*, she told herself. About half of the boxes in the attic qualified as small. Addie sighed and started with the closest stack. The first boxes held shoes, all outrageously outdated. The next stack was devoted to hat boxes, and Addie lost herself in the delight of trying on pill box hats, hats with veils, floppy straw hats, wide-brimmed hats. They were all old and stiff and smelled musty, but Addie didn't care.

Her favorite was a velvet one, royal blue, with a broad brim and silk ribbons that she tied under her chin. It had a fat bow at the nape of the neck with more silk ribbons that trailed down her back. She kept that one on and opened the next carton.

Here were the photo albums! Addie was amazed at her find and dug frantically through the next few boxes. All photo albums and old pictures. Where were those papers? It seemed logical that Gram would keep all the pictures and papers about the family in the same area. But there was still a stack of 10 or 15 more boxes and she was getting tired.

Then a shoebox with the words *GRANNY NOLDA* penciled on the side of it caught her attention. She pulled it from the stack and peered inside.

On top was a very old, very plain black leather book with the word *DIARY* barely visible. Under the diary was an odd assortment of paper. There were stationery pages, folded neatly, and columns of newspaper articles with words scribbled down the sides. Some pages were scraps torn haphazardly from a notebook. There were even several napkins with writing on them.

Addie picked up the piece of paper on top. It was pale yellow, no bigger than a bookmark, with one sentence written on it in very wobbly handwriting: *My grandmother told me about the first time she ever met a slave. NKE*

"This is it!" Addie cried out loud. She stuffed the paper and diary back in the box and slammed the lid on it all.

"Gram! Gram!" she shouted as she ran down the attic stairs with the box, hat ribbons flying behind her. "I think I found it!"

She swung fearlessly around the corner at the bottom of the attic stairs. The throw rug on the second floor landing slipped out from under her and the box flew from her grasp. Without warning, Addie tumbled headlong down the next flight of stairs and landed in a heap at the bottom. Gram's papers floated silently down behind her.

CHAPTER 3

Jacob and Daniel

Addie moaned softly. She could hear voices, but they all blended together and sounded slurred and far away. She opened her eyes, or thought she did, but nothing changed. Blobs of gray and white swirled around her.

"Addie?" Her father's voice broke through the jumble of sounds and she moaned again. "Honey, can you talk to me?"

Addie took a deep breath and shuddered. "Wow," she mumbled weakly.

"Thank You, Lord!" her dad said softly. "Okay, kiddo, don't move too fast. Just tell me if you can wiggle your fingers and your toes."

Addie suddenly realized she was curled in a tight little ball and she very gingerly began to stretch her legs and arms.

"Yeah, everything works," she finally murmured.

When she opened her eyes again, she could see her mom and Gram and Uncle Denny and some woman she didn't know. She couldn't see her dad, but she knew he was behind her, stroking her hair.

All the different heads seemed to bob up and down for several moments, then finally settled down on the shoulders of their respective owners. Addie blinked her eyes several times and smiled weakly at her mother.

"Oh, sweetheart," was all her mother said. She bit her lip and blinked back tears.

"Say, Peepunk, that was some tuck and roll you did there!" Uncle Denny's grin was strained. The strange woman reached out and worked first Addie's arms and then her legs. Finally, she looked Addie straight in the eye and studied her carefully.

"Are you a doctor?" Addie asked.

The pretty woman smiled. "A nurse," she answered and gave Uncle Denny a sideways glance.

Denny grinned. "Lucky I'm gonna marry her," he said. "She's already coming in handy."

Everyone laughed and Addie's eyes widened considerably. "Marry?!" she said. She struggled to sit up.

"Does your head hurt anywhere?" the woman asked. "Can you tell me if you hit it someplace in particular?"

"No," Addie said. "I was dizzy, but I'm okay now. My head doesn't hurt at all. It's this knee," she pointed to her right side, "and this wrist that hurt. I think I fell on them."

Her father nodded. "I saw you break your fall with that hand," he agreed.

"Well, nothing's broken," the nurse/fiancée said. "And there's no swelling at this point. We'll just wait and see. You'll probably be pretty sore, but that's all."

"Do we need to take her to the emergency room?" Addie's mom asked.

"No," answered Uncle Denny's fiancée. "Her pupils are back to normal already and she hasn't got any bumps we need to worry about."

"My head's fine," Addie repeated. A trip to the emergency room did not appeal to her. "I'm just sore. I'll be okay. Thanks," she added with a smile at the nurse. "Uh, what's your name?"

Uncle Denny smiled. "This is Linda Bedient, Peepunk, your almost-aunt."

"It's nice to meet you," Addie said shyly. "It'll be fun to have a new aunt."

"Thank you," Linda answered. "I'm looking forward to having a niece, too. Especially one that dresses so well!" She straightened the blue velvet hat that now sat at a crazy angle on Addie's head.

Everyone laughed again and with her father's help, Addie got to her feet. Then she saw the mess around her. Gram's box lay empty on the floor, the diary had been smashed beneath her and papers were everywhere.

"Oh, Gram, I'm so sorry!" she exclaimed.

Gram's face was still pale from the scare, but she gave her granddaughter a reassuring smile.

"No harm done, sweetie," she said. "Denny and Linda will help me pick this up. I think you had better get to bed."

She gave Addie a gentle kiss and hug, then shooed the three McCormicks up the stairs.

Addie's mother hovered over her while Addie changed her clothes and brushed her teeth. When she crawled in between the covers, both her parents sat down on the edge of the bed. Her father thanked God for protecting Addie and prayed especially that there wouldn't be any ill effects from her fall.

"I'm sorry," Addie told her parents when they were finished praying. "I should have been more careful."

"Yeah," her dad agreed, but he winked. "That's one way to learn a lesson."

"The hard way," Addie murmured. Her knee and wrist ached, but she didn't want to complain. She kissed her parents good night and they left the room. It was some time before Addie finally fell asleep.

* * *

When she woke up, sunlight was streaming through the window. She could hear the phone ringing downstairs, and the smell of bacon and eggs made her stomach rumble. Her mother's face appeared in the doorway.

"Finally!" Mrs. McCormick laughed. "Gram was just about ready to put the rest of the bacon back in the fridge."

"I'll be right there," Addie said. But when she tried to move, every muscle groaned, and she flopped back on her pillow.

"Sore?" her mom asked.

"Uh-huh," was all Addie said. *How could I have done such a stupid thing?* she chided herself. *Well, a few sore muscles aren't going to stop me!*

Once she began to move around, some of the soreness worked itself out. But her knee and wrist were still painful, though she tried not to show it. It took her longer than normal to get dressed and she couldn't walk down the stairs without limping.

Gram had a plate full of bacon and scrambled eggs waiting. Addie took a big slurp of orange juice and wolfed down two slices of bacon before she actually sat down.

"This is delicious, Gram!" she said with her mouth full.

"Addie!" her mom exclaimed.

"Good morning to you, too," Gram laughed.

"Sorry," Addie grinned. "But I was starved."

"You look like you're recovering nicely," Gram observed.

Addie only nodded. "Who was that on the phone?" she asked. "Uncle Jim or Uncle Lee?"

Gram bit her lip. "Uncle Lee," she finally answered. "They were coming for breakfast, but they're going to be late."

Gram's tone invited no more questions, but Addie's father ventured one anyway—the one they were all thinking.

"Jacob and Daniel at it again?"

Gram simply nodded.

Jake and Danny were Uncle Lee's two boys. Only 18 months apart in age, they were as different as boys could be. Danny was the oldest, athletic, outgoing, and not particularly studious, though he never had any real problems in school. He was a boy his father could understand.

Jacob was not. He had no real interest in anything related to sports, unless chess could be considered a sport. He had an insatiable curiosity and was always asking questions and taking things apart. He once spent six weeks designing and constructing a case that would protect an egg if you dropped it from a six-story building. It worked. He won the contest that was sponsored by the local university. Later, Uncle Lee told Addie's father he thought the whole thing was a waste of time and privately wondered how his youngest boy was going to make it in the "real world."

It was clear to Addie—and everyone else in the family—that Uncle Lee favored his oldest son. Daniel was a nice kid and Addie loved him like she loved all her cousins, but Jacob was her favorite.

For starters, they were "twin" cousins. Born on the same day, an hour apart, in different states, he was the closest thing Addie had to a brother. As they grew older, they even began to look alike. They had the same thick black hair and bright blue eyes, and people often thought they were siblings. It pleased both of them.

Whenever there was a family gathering, they spent every possible moment together. Addie had been looking forward to seeing Jacob again so soon after Christmas even though sibling rivalry between the boys had reared its ugly head in a serious way at Christmas. Rumors had been flying between family members ever since. Jacob and Daniel's fights were getting out of control.

Addie kept these thoughts to herself. *I'll keep Jake busy while they're here. If anyone can help me find this treasure, Jake can.*

"Say, Gram," Addie said between bites, "where did you put the letter and the key? And the box of papers? I wanted to start looking through them this morning."

"Right here," Gram answered, reaching on top of the microwave. "Why don't you take them to the study? That way you can spread them out without being in anyone's way. I'm afraid every other room is going to be occupied."

"Sure thing," Addie agreed. She finished her breakfast in a hurry, eager to get to her task.

The study was a large, warm room with an over-stuffed sofa, a coffee table, a rocking chair, lots of bookshelves, and two large desks. Addie decided to use her grandfather's desk since Gram's was covered with books and newspapers. When she sat down in his chair, a sudden ache of emotion constricted her throat. The room still smelled like Grandpa. She missed her grandfather very much and wondered briefly how much more Gram must miss him.

She put the antique box with the letter and key to one side. Then she sat the shoe box full of papers in front of her and took out the diary. It had been so squished by her fall, pages were bent every which way and the book no longer closed. She straightened out the pages as best she could, then stuck the whole thing under her grandfather's *Unabridged Webster's Dictionary* and hoped that it would flatten out.

Next she took out the simple family tree Gram had outlined. It told the maiden and married name of each of Addie's grandmothers, as well as their birthdate. She propped the family tree up against the lamp and took out the first piece of paper.

Mother remembers talk of treasure when she was little.
AEP

What did the letters AEP stand for? Addie remembered similar letters on the first note she read in the attic. A quick glance at other papers in the box showed letters at the end of each note.

Initials! Initials of the people who gave Gram the information. That must be—

The front door slammed with such force that Addie jumped.

"Listen, you little punk! I already told you I haven't seen your stupid book. Why would I care about weather patterns? You probably left it at the rest stop. Now leave me alone!"

"Gladly! I wish I could have left *you* at the rest stop!"

Jacob and Daniel had arrived.

CHAPTER 4

"Grandmama's Gold"

"Jacob, take your suitcase upstairs and stay there until you calm down. Daniel, in the kitchen." Uncle Lee's voice boomed through the house. Addie decided to stay put for a few minutes.

She went to Gram's typewriter and typed the initials of each grandmother next to their name on the family tree. That would make it easier to match them with the different notes in the box. She was not a fast typer, and it took her several minutes to get the job done.

When she finished, she took the paper and slipped upstairs to the room Jacob and Daniel always shared. She knocked softly.

"What?" came the sullen reply.

"Hi, Jake, it's me." Addie opened the door a crack and peered cautiously into the room.

The belligerent look on Jake's face disappeared at the sight of his favorite cousin. He put a finger to his lips, but motioned her inside. "Hi, Addie," he said softly. "Better not get caught in here. Dad'll accuse you of conspiring with the enemy."

"Oh, Jake," she said. "You're not the enemy."

"Tell my dad that," he said glumly.

Addie decided to change the subject. She handed Jake the family tree and he studied it curiously.

"What's this?" he asked.

"The names of all our grandmothers dating back to the Civil War. You're not going to believe what Gram gave me!"

For the next few minutes, Addie gave Jake a detailed account of the events of the previous night. When she came to the part about her tumble down the stairs, Jake gave her a teasing grin.

"Way to go, grace," he laughed.

Addie smiled sheepishly. "No kidding. I can't believe I did that myself. Anyway, Gram and Uncle Denny and Linda—have you met Linda?—picked everything up. I was going through it when you guys came. I'll show you everything when you—"

"When I break outta dis joint?" Jake finished the sentence for her in his best gangster voice and Addie laughed.

Jake studied the family tree with renewed interest. "So what do you hope to find in Gram's notes?"

"Something that will tell me what this key opens!"

Jake frowned. "It would help to know what the treasure is. That might narrow down the options for what the key opens."

That made sense. Jake always made sense. "Will you help me?" Addie asked.

"Of course," Jake grinned, but his smile faded quickly. "Better scoot!" There were footsteps on the stairs and Addie dove off the bed and ran for the door.

Her room was right across the hall. She paused inside her door for several seconds, then came out again just as Uncle Lee came to the top of the landing.

"Hi, Uncle Lee," she said and gave him a hug.

"Hi, Peepunk," he said quietly. "It's good to see you."

"You, too," she answered.

"How's Jake doing in there?" he asked.

"He's okay—" the words were hardly out of her mouth before she realized her mistake.

Uncle Lee only smiled and winked. "Get on downstairs. Aunt Jenny wants to see you."

Lee and Jacob joined the family in the living room several minutes later. Jake went directly to his brother.

"I'm sorry," he said briefly.

Daniel shrugged. "S'okay. Me too."

Everyone else in the room heard the exchange, but pretended not to. Several conversations struck up at the same time, and Jake joined Addie on the sofa.

"So where's this letter and key?" he asked.

"The study. Come on," she said and led the way to the back room.

Jake pulled Gram's chair next to Addie's at the desk. He read the letter silently several times over before he finally looked up.

"Does this make any sense to you?" he asked Addie.

"Not much."

"First of all," he said, "who's Winnie?"

Addie pointed to the name at the top of the family tree. "The first woman in our family to name her daughter Addie." She briefly explained the "gram plus" system to him. "Gram plus four, Winnie's daughter, was named after this woman." She pointed to the name at the bottom of the letter.

"Okay." Jake studied the letter once more. "What does she mean by 'the scope of events that occurred in our country in the last week?'" he asked "The treasure is related to those events."

Addie frowned. "Is there a date?" she asked.

Jake nodded. "Yep. November 9, 1860. What happened in 1860?"

Addie shrugged, then snapped her fingers. "The Civil War was—"

"Nope." Jake interrupted her. "The war didn't really start until 1861." He went back to the letter. "And what does *portent* mean?"

"It's like a prediction, or a foreshadowing, of things to come. The treasure isn't a prediction of what Addie's future is going to be." She was glad she could answer at least one of Jake's questions.

"So the way this sounds, the treasure puts the baby Addie in the shadow of great men, but the adult Addie wants her to follow in their footsteps, not be in their shadow." Jake gave a short laugh and tossed the letter on the desk. "I'm lost."

"Don't say that, Jake!" Addie pleaded. "I really need your help."

"Well, I don't think we should start with that letter," he said.

So Addie pulled the pile of papers from the shoe box. She and Jake read the first three or four notes carefully. They checked the source for each and tried to find a way to organize the information they were reading.

"This is going way too slow," Jake finally said. "Tell you what. Let's each take a few of these notes and skim the information. We'll put them in categories later. Save anything that has a reference to the treasure and we'll check those first. Okay?"

Addie agreed. For the next half hour they read silently. In the end, they found only three notes that mentioned the treasure directly. One was the piece Addie had found earlier that morning. *Mother remembers talk of treasure when she was little. AEP* The others said, *Mama's treasure escaped the fire. NKE* and *We must get the treasure back, the fire is over. NKE*

Addie studied the family tree. "Okay. AEP is Adlon Elder Powell. Her mother remembers talk of treasure when she was little. Her mother is Nolda Kelley Elder—NKE. She's the one who's talking about the fire." She looked at Jake in frustration. "*What* fire?"

Jake shrugged. "Who knows?"

"Wait a minute!" Addie consulted the family tree again. "Look. AEP was Gram's grandmother. Maybe Gram knows about the fire. Let's ask!"

They raced to the kitchen where everyone was busy fixing lunch. Gram and Uncle Denny were opening the big table in the dining room and Addie's father was carrying in table leaves.

"Gram, look at these!" Addie waved the papers under Gram's nose and her father gave her a warning look

"Wait till Gram's finished, kiddo," he said.

"Sorry." Addie backed away until the table was stretched from end to end of the dining room. Then she asked, "Do you remember anything about a fire, Gram?"

Gram looked down her nose through her bifocals and studied the papers carefully. "Oh, yes." She shook her head sadly.

"Granny Nolda was my great-grandmother. Her family had a very bad fire when she was a young woman. The whole house burned, although they managed to salvage a few things. My goodness." Gram's eyes widened. "That was more than a hundred years ago. Isn't that amazing? Anyway, when I began to look into the treasure, Granny Nolda was in her eighties and her mind was very feeble. Whenever I asked her about the treasure, she got very agitated and told me it was safe from the fire, but we had to get it back. No one understood what she meant."

"You knew your great-grandmother?" Jake was incredulous.

Gram nodded. "She outlived my mother and my grandmother. Most of the women in our family had their first child at a fairly young age, so it wasn't unusual for us to span four, sometimes five, generations."

"Do you know anything else about Granny Nolda's childhood or the fire?" Addie asked.

Gram shook her head. "No. But you have her diary. Why don't you check that?"

"That's Nolda's diary?"

Gram nodded.

"Let's go, Jake." Addie headed for the door, but her mother stopped her.

"Check after lunch, Addie. We need someone to set the table. Would you and Jake help?"

Addie heaved a sigh, but nodded reluctantly. "How many places?" she asked.

"Ten," said Gram.

Together she and Jake had the table set in record time, hoping to get back to the study and the diary. But Aunt Jenny and Gram followed them around the table with platters of sandwiches, fried potatoes, and two big bowls of fruit salad, so lunch began immediately.

Meals at Gram's were always a wonderful event. Soon Addie and Jake forgot their eagerness to get to the diary and were laughing and joking with the rest of the family. Even Daniel was in a good mood. He seemed eager to make amends for the morning argument.

"You two want to walk downtown and see a movie this afternoon?" he asked Jake and Addie.

Jake responded before Addie had a chance. "No thanks," he said. "Addie and I are busy." He went on to tell Daniel the details of their search for clues to the family treasure, but Daniel didn't seem interested. He left the table soon afterward.

"Maybe Daniel could help us look through the papers," she suggested to Jake when his brother was gone. "I think you hurt his feelings."

Jake wrinkled his nose. "Are you kidding? Nothing bothers him."

But Uncle Lee agreed with Addie and said so when they excused themselves from the table. "That was Danny's way of making up with you, Jake. Can't you even meet him halfway?"

Jake was perplexed. "But—I don't *want* to go to a movie, Dad."

Uncle Lee just shook his head and waved them out of the room.

"What did I do wrong?" Jake asked Addie the rhetorical question when they got to the study. "It doesn't matter what I do, I can't win. I give up."

"Well, let's just forget about it for a while," Addie said. "Why don't you go through those papers again and try to organize them, and I'll go through Granny Nolda's diary and see what I can find."

For the next hour they read quietly. Occasionally Jake would look up from his work and ask, "Find anything?" The answer was always no.

But Addie learned a great many other things about her gram plus three. The diary began in 1888, when Nolda was only 11 years old. She was an outspoken young thing and gave her opinion freely on a variety of topics, from the neighbor girl's new "beau" to the color of dress that looked best on the preacher's wife.

She was also given to impromptu prayers, written in bold letters and underlined. They were usually plopped right in the middle of a lengthy discourse on any given topic. Addie read her favorite one to Jake.

"'*Mary Kate's freckles are popping out all over again this summer. I cannot understand why that girl's mother*

*doesn't teach her the proper manner of dress for young
women, especially in the hot sun. **Thank You, dear Lord,
for delivering me from the curse of freckles. May I
always be blessed with clear skin. And if it be in Your
will, Lord, deliver Mary Kate as well.'"**

Jacob hooted with laughter at the "curse" of
freckles, but stopped when he saw the look on
Addie's face. "What is it?"

"Listen to this!" Addie's voice was hoarse with
excitement.

"'Today Mama showed me her treasures and told me
the story of Grandmama's gold. She said she had news
clippings, but we can't find them now. Mama does need to
be more organized.'"*

CHAPTER 5

The Search Begins

When Gram saw the entry in the diary, her eyes sparkled with excitement. "'*Mama's treasure and Grandmama's gold*,'" she repeated several times. "I knew you could do it, Addie!"

"Gram," Addie protested, "we haven't done anything yet."

"You've gotten farther than I ever did—in just one day." Gram gave both her grandchildren a quick squeeze before she went back to the diary. "I never knew there was gold involved!"

"But it doesn't sound as if the treasure and the gold are the same thing," Addie pointed out. "Nolda says the treasure belongs to 'Mama,' who was the first Adlon, and the gold belongs to 'Grandmama,' whose name was Winnie Johnson Haile."

"That's true," Gram said thoughtfully. "I wonder what happened to the news clippings she talked about?"

"Maybe the clippings tell about the fire," Addie suggested.

Gram shook her head. "I don't think so. The fire occurred several years later—when Nolda was engaged to be married. They must tell the story of the gold."

"I've read through the clippings in the box," Jake said. "None of them mention gold or treasure at all. They're all obituaries."

Addie grimaced. "Why do people save things like obituaries? It makes me sad to read about how people died."

Gram smiled tenderly. "As odd as it sounds, honey, it's a part of life. And keeping a history of the lives and deaths of your loved ones can bring you great comfort.

"But," Gram cleared her throat and went back to the diary, "what was the story behind the treasure and the gold? Were they connected somehow?"

"And why would they have news clippings about them?" Jake added. "And where could we get a copy of the clippings?"

Addie took the diary from Jake. Granny Nolda had been sporadic in her writing. It was not a daily process, and she seldom included dates. Addie checked back through the early pages and found the last date prior to the entry about the treasure.

"July 7, 1889," she said. "Maybe we could go to the library and check the local newspapers from the year 1889."

"Better ask your folks first," Gram suggested.

Their parents agreed to the trip and Uncle Denny volunteered to drop them off at the library. He and Linda were going with Daniel to a movie.

The library was an old, squat brick building that sprawled across half a city block. Inside everything was very modern. Plush carpet muffled any noise, and the librarian's station was set on a platform in the very center of a large, open room. It looked like a small boat adrift in a sea of books.

Addie and Jake approached the librarian and told her about their project. She listened with interest.

"I hope we can help you," she said. "We keep material that old on microfilm in the archives. The archives are in the basement." She pointed to a nondescript door marked STAIRS. "There's a reference librarian on duty, but she doesn't get much traffic down there, so you might have to look for her."

Addie and Jake ran down the stairs and went through another door propped open with a box. The basement seemed much darker because there were no windows, but it was still well-lit and filled with books. There was no one at the desk, so the two children walked up and down several aisles, searching for the librarian.

There seemed to be no one else in the archives and the silence became eerie. Addie giggled nervously.

"We're probably the only customers she's had this decade," Jake whispered. "Maybe she skipped out years ago, and everyone just thinks she's down here doing her job."

"May I help you?" A clear, soft voice seemed to come out of nowhere, and Addie and Jake both jumped. They turned to find a very pretty young woman regarding them with an amused expression on her face.

"Uh, sorry," Jake murmured. "We weren't sure there was anyone down here."

"Well, here I am," she smiled. "What can I help you with?"

Addie explained their project once more and the young woman—her name was Joanna—was fascinated with their story.

"What an interesting family history!" she exclaimed. "I'm sure we have copies of the paper from that year. It's all on microfilm."

She soon had Addie and Jake set up at a desk with the microfilm machine. She brought out reels for the entire year and showed how to insert them.

They began with the January 1 edition and scrolled through each page of the paper, trying to scan the headlines for any mention of gold or Winnie Johnson Haile. It was a tedious process. By the time they reached the last edition of the paper for January 1889, more than an hour had passed.

"This isn't going to work," Jake finally said, totally discouraged.

Addie shut off the projector and rubbed her tired eyes. "I agree."

"We need more information, something more specific to look for," he said. "We'll have to go back to the diary and see if Nolda gives any more information about those news clippings."

They watched an elderly man with a cart full of cleaning supplies come out of a door at the far end of the room. Joanna joined him and together they rolled the cart into a small utility room. The man donned his coat and Joanna bid him a quiet good night.

Addie rolled her head in little circles, trying to work out the kinks in her neck. "We should have done that in the first place, I guess. I'm going to be real mad at myself if we read that Nolda found the news clippings the next day."

They gathered up all the films and returned them to the desk. Joanna was disappointed too. "I really hoped you'd find what you were looking for," she said.

Jake laughed. "We don't *know* what we're looking for."

"Well, if you figure it out, please come back. I'd like to help you if I can."

The children browsed through the juvenile section of the library until five o'clock. Then they met Denny, Linda, and Daniel at the ice cream shop down the street. Daniel was eating a large chocolate sundae.

"So, Sherlock, what clues did you two sleuths uncover about the family treasure?" Daniel deepened his voice on the last two words, and Jake frowned at the teasing tone.

"We didn't find anything," he said shortly.

"Shoulda gone to the movie like I suggested," Daniel replied. "You wasted a whole afternoon in the library."

"Yeah, right," Jake said sarcastically. "The library is such a waste of time. I wish I could have watched some walking advertisement for steroids get all his appendages blown off. That would have been *very* enlightening."

Daniel's eyes narrowed and he glared at his younger brother. "Uncle Denny loved it," he said.

Jake glanced quickly at his uncle and bit his lip to keep from saying anything more.

"Don't drag me into your argument," Uncle Denny protested. "Just drop it, okay?"

They both nodded.

"Either of you want any ice cream?" Linda asked.

Addie got a small cone, but Jake wasn't hungry. The ride home was a quiet one.

When they entered the kitchen, Gram looked up from the soup she was making. "Any luck?" she asked.

Addie just shook her head.

"How was the movie?" Uncle Lee asked his oldest son.

Daniel gave Jake a defiant stare. "Enlightening," he said and left the room.

Supper consisted of Gram's vegetable soup and homemade bread. Addie loved Gram's bread and almost always ate too much. Tonight was no exception. She dunked big chunks of it in her soup and when she was finished with that, she slathered blackberry jelly on another slice for dessert. She was the last to finish eating, which meant it was her job to clear the table. She didn't care. Gram's bread was worth it.

After dishes were done, Uncle Denny suggested a game of charades. They all sat in the living room and acted out movie and book titles and famous names and places. Daniel wasn't very good at the game and soon he dropped out and left the room.

Jake excused himself several minutes later. Addie didn't think much about it until she heard loud voices. They were coming from the study. Uncle Lee heard the voices too and closed his eyes wearily. Then he got to his feet and walked down the hall to the far end of the house.

Everyone else grew quiet as the argument intensified.

"He's messing in Addie's stuff!" came Jake's voice. "That's none of his business!"

"Hey, it's my family, too. I just wanted to see what all this mystery stuff was about. What's wrong with that?"

The door to the study closed and the voices dimmed. The game of charades resumed, but no one's heart was in it, and they called it quits when Addie guessed the movie—*Gone with the Wind*. Someone switched on the TV and Gram, Aunt Jenny, and Addie's mom went back to the kitchen for coffee. Denny and Linda went to the piano, and Linda played while Uncle Denny and Addie's father sang old hymns. Normally Addie would have joined them, but tonight she stretched out on the sofa and closed her eyes. She listened to the soothing harmony that came from years of singing together.

Uncle Lee came back into the room. "Jake said to tell you good night," he whispered to Addie. "He and Daniel are going to bed early."

"Okay," she whispered back. He turned away, but Addie touched his arm and he looked down at her. "Uncle Lee, I don't care if Daniel looks at Gram's papers. It *is* his family treasure—as much as it is mine."

Uncle Lee ruffled her hair gently. "Thanks, honey. But the problem really isn't about Gram's papers."

Addie nodded. "I know."

Uncle Lee joined his brothers and added his deep bass to the singing. Their voices blended perfectly and there was a quiet camaraderie between the three brothers that went beyond the words they sang.

Addie's eyes suddenly filled with tears. How did they grow to be so close? And why couldn't Jacob and Daniel develop that kind of friendship?

She got up off the sofa and crossed the room to kiss her father good night. Then she stuck her head in the kitchen door.

"I'm going to bed, Mom," she said.

"I'll be up in a few minutes, honey," her mother answered.

Addie stopped by the study to pick up Granny Nolda's diary before she went upstairs. She changed her clothes and brushed her teeth then got the diary and crawled into bed. Her mom came in and prayed with her. As always, she seemed to know just what was on Addie's heart.

"Lord," she said, "we want to pray tonight for Jacob and Daniel. Father, they're so different, but they are both precious to You. I pray that even at this young age, they could begin to look past their differences, and learn to appreciate the strengths of the other.

"And Lord, if it's Your will, give Addie the wisdom and insight she needs to be a buffer between them. Show her ways to draw them closer together. It's a lot to ask, Lord, but You're a big God. Thank You for Your answers to all our needs, and bless Addie with a good night's sleep. In Jesus' name, Amen."

Addie kissed her mother good night. She was too tired to read the diary, so she set it on the nightstand and turned out the light.

A buffer between them, huh? she thought sleepily. *Sounds uncomfortable to me.*

CHAPTER 6

The Gold Rush

Addie brought the diary with her when she came downstairs for breakfast Thursday morning. Jake was already at the table eating. Gram set a platter of French toast on the table, and Addie helped herself to three slices. Jake took two more, doused them in maple syrup, and passed the syrup to Addie.

"So where do we start this morning?" he asked by way of greeting.

"Why don't you start with an hour's worth of homework?" Uncle Lee suggested.

Addie's mom was washing dishes at the sink and heard his comment. "Good idea," she agreed. "I know Addie has quite a bit to do."

Addie and Jake exchanged frustrated glances, but neither argued. When they were finished with breakfast, they carried their dishes to the sink then found their school books and retired to the study.

Addie took Gram's desk and worked on math problems while Jake sat in Grandpa's rocking chair and read his book on weather patterns. Daniel joined them a few minutes later and stretched out on the sofa with a history text. He glanced at the book Jake was reading, but said nothing.

For the next hour, the children read or worked silently. The only noise was the occasional bang of a pot or pan being put away in the kitchen. Addie was almost finished with her math assignment when she looked out the study window and saw Uncle Jim's van pull into the drive. Before the van came to a complete stop, the side door banged open and three little bodies tumbled out.

"So much for peace and quiet," Daniel muttered, but he said it with a grin. Addie and Jake both shut their books and together the three children left the study and went to the front door to greet their younger cousins.

Uncle Jim was the last of the four brothers to arrive at Gram's for the weekend. He and Aunt Bev had four children—Christopher was eight, Abraham was four, Evan was three, and baby Lindsey was not quite two months. All things considered, the three boys were very well-behaved kids. But everyone knew Aunt Bev was ecstatic to have a little girl.

Abraham was Addie's special pal and he searched the sea of familiar faces until he found hers. Then he disappeared into the maze of legs and came out at her side.

"Hold me, Addie," he commanded and she obligingly picked him up, even though it hurt her wrist. For her effort she got a very wet kiss that smelled suspiciously like Oreos.

"Abe," she said with a laugh, "have you been eating cookies?"

His joyous smile gave proof he had indeed been eating cookies and he whispered loudly, "Breakfast!"

Aunt Bev blushed at her child's revelation, but she only shrugged. "We left so early this morning, no one was hungry. I thought we'd get here before breakfast. When we didn't, Abe and Evan got cranky, so I let them eat the Oreos. I figured it wouldn't kill 'em."

Aunt Bev had a very relaxed attitude when it came to kids and food, and Addie felt a slight twinge of envy. Oreos for breakfast would have sent her mother into a tizzy.

Gram took baby Lindsey from Uncle Jim. The rest of the family oohed and aahed over the newest member of the family and the adults gravitated toward the kitchen for more coffee. Soon only the children were left standing in the front entry.

"Whatcha been doin', Addie?" Abe asked.

"We're solving a mystery, Abe," she answered. "You want to help?"

"Yeah!" Abe crowed with delight.

"Me, too." Christopher frowned at his little brother. "I'm bigger. I can help better'n you."

"Eban, too," said the littlest one and pulled at Addie's pant leg.

Jacob swooped Evan off his feet and the boy giggled. "You can all help," he said. "Come on. We'll show you the mystery letter and the key."

Jake swung Evan onto his shoulders and Addie led the way to the study. Evan squirmed around to look back down the hall. "Come on, Danny," he called. "You wanna hep?"

Addie grinned back at her oldest cousin. "Yeah, Danny, we need your 'hep'!" Daniel joined the rest of the cousins.

Once in the study, Addie read the letter to the three little boys. Christopher listened with great interest, but Abe's attention was distracted by the big key, and Evan started doing headstands on the sofa.

"Now," Jacob said when Addie was finished, "it's very important that no one touches this letter or key, or this box of papers. Only Addie and," he paused slightly, "Daniel, and I can touch these things."

"Jacob, I'm eight years old." Christopher was slightly disgusted.

"I know you are, Chris, but ... it's very important that you set an example for the little boys. You have to show them how important it is to leave the letter and key and stuff where it's at. Okay?"

Christopher nodded solemnly. "I will, Jake," he promised. To his brothers he said, "Touch those and you're dead meat."

Daniel snickered and Addie stooped to give Abe and Evan a little hug. "We trust you," she reassured them, though it was hard to keep from laughing.

Evan made a face at his oldest brother and Abe stuck his tongue out at Christopher. Chris made a fist with his right hand and Evan ducked behind Addie.

"This is just great," Addie muttered. "Now I've got to keep *five* different brothers from killing one another."

Daniel and Jacob exchanged embarrassed glances and Daniel changed the subject. "You'd better explain exactly what we're doing," he said.

"I bet we're looking for that treasure in the letter," Christopher said.

"What treasure? Who gots a treasure?" Evan suddenly joined the conversation.

"Is this a key to a treasure chest?" Abe reached out and almost touched the key but Christopher smacked his hand.

"You're not gonna get a thing done with these two around," Chris informed his older cousins.

As if on cue, Uncle Jim opened the door to the study. "Hey guys, who wants some breakfast? Gram has French toast."

Abe and Evan practically knocked one another over in their haste to get down to the kitchen, but Christopher hung back.

"Can I come back when I'm finished?"

"Sure, Chris." Addie smiled kindly at the little boy, and he left the room with a bounce in his step.

The three older children looked at one another. "We better work fast," Jake declared.

"I'll skim through the rest of the diary and see if I can find anything more about the news clippings or the fire," Addie said.

"I'll go back to organizing these notes," Jake decided. He hesitated. "You want to help me, Daniel?"

"Sure," Daniel said. "Just tell me what I'm looking for."

Jake summed up their progress so far. "Nolda's diary mentions the first time she heard about Adlon's

treasure and Winnie's gold. We think they're connected, but we don't know how. The only other
information we have about the treasure comes from
Gram's notes." He showed Daniel the papers with
the initials NKE at the end. "When Nolda was old,
she told Gram the treasure was safe from the fire,
but she had to get it back. Gram said Nolda was
kind of whacked-out by that time and no one knew
what she meant."

Daniel looked skeptical. "Gram said she was
'whacked-out'?"

"No," Addie frowned at Jake. "She said her
'mind was feeble.'"

Jake shrugged. "Anyway, we need to look for
anything that tells us more about the treasure, the
gold, or the fire. Okay?"

Daniel nodded. He took a handful of notes and
stretched out on the sofa once more.

Christopher was back sooner than any of them
expected. "The little kids are going to the grocery
store with Dad and Uncle John," he informed
them. "What can I do?" he asked Jake eagerly.

Jake studied his earnest face and took a deep
breath. "Well, can you read?"

Christopher stood up straight and looked Jake
right in the eye. "Of course I can read," he said in a
highly offended tone. "I'm the best reader in third
grade."

"Great," Jake said. "The treasure was lost after a
fire. Read these letters and tell me if they say anything about the treasure or gold or a fire." He gave
Christopher two letters written on blue stationery.

The little boy sat down on the floor, Indian-style, and began reading.

Addie's search through the diary revealed nothing more. Although Granny Nolda made several references to "Mama's story" and "Grandmama's gold," she never included details. The diary stopped before the fire occurred. Addie was puzzled.

"Why wouldn't she write about the treasure in her diary?" she wondered. "She writes about everything else. It almost seems like the treasure wasn't important to her."

Christopher nodded solemnly. "I only put important things in my journal," he said. "Secrets."

"*You* keep a journal?" Addie was amazed, but Jake looked at his young cousin thoughtfully.

"He's got a point, you know. The treasure wasn't a secret to anyone then. It was only a gift to Nolda's mother. That's probably not something a girl would put in her diary."

"But what about the gold?" Addie persisted. "Surely that would be important to her."

Jake shrugged. "If the story about the gold was common knowledge in the family, why would she write about it?"

"You'd think *someone* would want to keep a written record of how they got it," she said.

"Maybe they just found the gold," Christopher suggested helpfully.

"Chris, people don't just 'find' gold," Jake said impatiently.

The younger boy got a stubborn look in his eye. "My teacher said a lot of people found gold. It was in the old days and there was a big hurry to find it."

Daniel grinned. "He's talking about the Gold Rush."

Christopher's expression brightened considerably. "That's it—the Gold Rush."

"Okay, you're right, Chris," Jake conceded. "People did find gold back then. But that was in California. This is Wisconsin."

"Maybe they went to California to find it." Christopher was not going to be deterred.

Daniel was staring intently at his young cousin. "Maybe they did . . ." he said thoughtfully.

Jake shot his older brother a look that said, *Why are you encouraging this?* but Daniel didn't notice. He was busy digging through the notes he had been reading. Addie and Jake both winced.

"Dan, be careful!" Jake complained. "Some of those papers are real old."

"Yeah, yeah, yeah," Daniel muttered. Then he found what he was looking for and held up a very old piece of newspaper. "Listen to this!"

"What is it?" Addie asked.

"An obituary for . . . Samuel Elder," he answered, "but that's not important."

Addie consulted the family tree. "Samuel Elder was Nolda's husband."

"Great," Danny said shortly, "but that's not important. *This* is." He began reading. "'Mr. Elder's death from drowning is the third such tragedy to befall Mrs. Elder's family in as many generations. Her father, Randolph Kelley—'"

He paused and looked at Addie. She checked the family tree and nodded.

Daniel continued. "'—Randolph Kelley, died in a boating accident in 1899. Her grandfather, Harrison Haile—'" Addie nodded again "'—died at sea in 1858.'"

"Harrison Haile was Winnie's husband," Addie said slowly.

"He must have left Wisconsin at some point," Daniel said. "There aren't too many seas he could have drowned in around here!"

"Which sea?" Jacob asked sensibly.

Daniel shrugged. "Doesn't say. But—there's more." He reached under the sofa and pulled out his history text. "We studied about the Gold Rush last semester." He fanned through the first few chapters of the book, muttering to himself.

Jake couldn't stand it. "Check the index," he said impatiently.

Daniel frowned at him. *"Check the index,"* he mimicked, but did as he was told and found what he was looking for in short order. He skimmed the material quickly.

"Listen." He began to read from the text. "'Although many miners chose to remain in California to add to their hoard of gold, others were content to take their fortunes home. It was impractical, difficult, and dangerous to transport great quantities of gold across the continental United States, so most miners chose to travel from coast to coast by way of the sea. Even this mode of travel was not without its perils. There were occasional reports of nineteenth-century pirates, but more common was man's battle

with Mother Nature. High winds and even hurri-
canes often beset the travelers and more than one
ship was known to give up its bounty to the sea.'"

Daniel looked up from his reading. "What do
you think?"

Jacob still looked skeptical.

"Jake, it says right here the Gold Rush hit its peak
in the late 1850s. We know Winnie Haile had gold.
We know her husband died at sea, and we know
there were news clippings about the gold. Maybe
the clippings told about a shipwreck. I think it
makes sense," Daniel said defiantly.

Addie felt a small tingle of excitement run up her
spine. She gave Jacob a friendly poke and he grinned
reluctantly.

"Might as well check it out," he agreed.

"All right!" Daniel beamed. "Good detective work,
Christopher." He held out his hand, palm up, and
Christopher slapped it hard, grinning from ear to
ear.

CHAPTER 7

Back to the Library

"Let's run our theory by Gram first," Addie suggested.

"Good idea," Jacob agreed.

They found Gram in the living room, rocking her youngest grandchild. The baby was wide awake and making soft, mewing sounds, waving her arms and staring wide-eyed around her. It was hard to get Gram's attention.

"A shipwreck?" Gram finally took her eyes off the baby and concentrated on her four oldest grandchildren. "Who is it you think died in a shipwreck?"

Daniel showed her the obituary. "Harrison Haile died at sea."

"And two other men in our family drowned as well," Addie said.

Gram snapped her fingers. "You're right. Now I remember. Granny Nolda was scared to death of the water. She said it took the only two men she ever loved—her husband and her father. She never knew Harrison Haile, of course. But she knew he died at sea. She even told me the name of the ship. I wrote it down in my notes somewhere. Haven't you found it yet?"

Jacob and Addie looked at one another. "I don't think there's any mention of a ship, Gram," Addie said. "None that I remember, anyway."

"Well, you'd better look again," she said. "I'm sure I wrote it down somewhere. If you can't find it, we'll call Uncle Ed. He has a wonderful memory. If he ever heard the story, I'm sure he could tell you the name."

Ed was not really an uncle, but Gram's cousin, and the best friend Grandpa McCormick had ever had. The two men were in the same company during World War II. When Ed came home on furlough one holiday, he brought his friend, Ken McCormick, with him. Gram was six years younger than Ken McCormick, but she fell in love with the handsome soldier and the rest was history.

A thorough search of the shoe box and its contents produced no mention of a ship, so Gram made the call to Uncle Ed herself and invited Ed and his wife Lizzy to lunch. Aunt Lizzy wasn't feeling well, but Uncle Ed was at the kitchen door half an hour later.

He arrived the same time Addie's father, Uncle Jim, and the two little boys returned from their excursion to the grocery store. They had stopped at a fried chicken joint on the way home, and soon the dining room table was filled with red and white buckets of steaming chicken as well as little white containers of coleslaw and potatoes with gravy.

Lunch was a casual affair, with paper plates and napkins, while the whole family listened to Addie and Jacob's story of their search for the treasure. Daniel and Chris told how they believed Harrison Haile might have been prospecting for gold in California.

When they finished, Uncle Lee beamed at his oldest son. "That's pretty good deductive reasoning," he said.

Daniel just grinned, and Jacob stared silently at his plate.

Addie saw the look on Jake's face and changed the subject. "Can you remember the name of the ship, Uncle Ed?" she asked.

Ed frowned. "I'm afraid not. I don't believe I ever heard the name," he said. "I remember vague references to Harrison Haile's death, but nothing that specific. I'm sure an event of that magnitude would be in the local papers, though. I'd say you'd best get back to the library and do some more research. I can drop you off there on my way home, if you like."

Young Abraham clapped his hands. "I love the liberry," he said and gave Addie a huge grin.

Addie smiled back but took a deep breath. Jake and Daniel looked everywhere but at the little boy. Christopher, however, made no effort to be tactful.

"You're not going with us," he said bluntly.

Abe's bottom lip began to tremble and Evan sniffled pitifully. Chris knew a snow job when he saw one and he turned quickly to his mother.

"Mom!" he wailed, but she held up a hand and pointed to his father.

"Now, Chris," Uncle Jim began, but Jake interrupted him.

"The library has a great children's section," he said to Addie and Daniel. "We could take turns watching them upstairs."

"That's very kind of you, Jake," Aunt Bev smiled. "Thanks."

Abe and Evan both cheered wildly. Christopher knew it was pointless to argue, so he began laying down the rules even as they left the room to get their coats.

"There's not a pop machine in the library, so don't even ask," he told Evan. "And we're not gonna take you to the bathroom every five minutes, you understand?" Abe nodded. "We've got work to do . . ."

His voice faded down the hall and the adults laughed quietly. Uncle Lee pulled Jacob to one side. "Remember you're the one responsible for this. Don't complain when it's your turn to watch them. Don't make Danny do all the work."

Jake shrugged out of his father's grasp. "It was my idea, Dad," he said sharply. "Don't worry about it."

Uncle Lee frowned at the tone in Jacob's voice, but he simply nodded. "Call when you're ready to come home. One of us will pick you up."

The six children bundled up against the bitter cold and piled into Uncle Ed's large, black Continental. Christopher and Daniel sat in front while Addie and Jake took the back, with Abe and Evan squished into one seat belt between them. Jake stared silently out the window until they got to the library.

Once inside, he offered to take the first watch upstairs. "Show Chris and Daniel the archives," he said. "Just send someone up to relieve me in about 20 minutes, okay?"

Addie led her two cousins down the stairs. Joanna was at her desk and she was delighted to see Addie again.

"Where's Jake?" she asked.

"Upstairs, watching my little brothers," Chris told her. "We gotta take turns."

Joanna tried to hide her smile at the obvious disgust in Christopher's voice. "What are you looking for today?" she asked Addie.

When Addie told her they needed the microfilm for newspapers from the year 1858, her smile faded quickly.

"I'm afraid our collection is very sparse before the year 1860," she said reluctantly. "I'll show you what we have, but it's not much. I guess no one thought to save the newspapers before the Civil War. The copies we have on film came from private collections."

This time there was only one canister of microfilm. Addie took it to the machine and inserted the film carefully. She began to scroll through the first paper saved from 1858. It was dated March 13.

"What if he died before March 13?" Daniel asked.

"We're out of luck," Addie answered.

She scrolled to the obituaries first. No Harrison Haile. She went back to the front page and examined each headline carefully. Nothing. There were only four more papers from March 1858. After a two-month gap, the next paper was dated June 11.

"It's going to be a miracle if we find the article that tells about his death," Daniel said.

Silently, Addie agreed, but she continued to scroll through each paper carefully. The process seemed even slower than it had the day before. More than an hour passed.

"Jake!" Daniel said suddenly. He picked up his coat and headed upstairs. Jake came down in less than a minute and Addie explained the problem. He took over the microfilm while Addie rested her eyes.

Christopher got tired soon afterward and decided to help Daniel upstairs. "You don't have to relieve me," he told Addie. "I don't want to do this anymore. It's boring."

Addie agreed, but she thanked him anyway. She and Jake were left alone to finish reading the few newspapers that were left. Daniel had evidently decided to stay upstairs with the boys.

About 20 minutes later, Joanna came over to check their progress. "No luck, right?" she asked.

"Right," Jake said. "I don't think we're going to find anything."

"I know there are public records of the shipwrecks that have occurred in U.S. waters over the years," Joanna said. "We can get that information and pull out the names of ships that sank during 1858. It will take some time, but it can be done."

"Excuse me, Joanna." The janitor Jake and Addie had seen the day before spoke softly from the far end of the room. "I'm taking these garbage bags out to the dumpster. Let me back in when I knock, will you?"

Joanna nodded and waved, and the man heaved one bag over his shoulder and picked up two more in his right hand.

"What's he doing?" Jake asked.

Joanna laughed ruefully. "We're trying to catalog and clean out everything in the storage rooms. I took this job six months ago and we still have one room left to clean. The last few librarians saved every book or magazine or piece of paper they ever got their hands on. The problem is, they marked it 'Archives' and stuck it here in the basement. No one has looked in those rooms for years."

She checked the microfilm in the machine. "You're almost finished with this," she said. "Scroll through the last few papers just to assure yourself you didn't miss anything. Then I'll go upstairs with you and see if we can't find *something* on shipwrecks in 1858."

Addie and Jake finished their search in less than 15 minutes. They took the reel back to Joanna's desk. She was busy typing a list, but said she would join them when she finished.

The two children trudged up the stairs to the main floor. They could see Daniel and Evan stretched out on the floor in the children's section, putting together an elaborate puzzle of alphabetical zoo animals. Christopher sat next to them reading a book.

Daniel looked up when they approached. "I knew you wouldn't find anything," he said without even asking.

"Look, Addie," Evan said. "We gots a zebra and a kangaroo and a hippo and a plink flaminko . . . a plink famingo . . . a . . ." The other children's laughter drowned out his attempts to pronounce the name and he shrugged cheerfully. "One of those," he said, pointing to the graceful bird.

"A pink flamingo," Addie corrected him gently, then looked around. "Where's Abe?"

Daniel glanced up from his work. "Did you take him to the bathroom?" he asked Chris.

Chris looked shocked. "I thought you took him," he said.

"Great," Daniel muttered. He stood up and stretched his legs. "Come on, we have to find him. He's got to be here somewhere."

Addie took Evan with her and the children split up to search, but the little boy was nowhere to be found.

CHAPTER 8

Lost
in the Library

The children stood in a small, frightened clump, blocking the entrance to the play area for preschoolers. Jacob scanned the huge library once more. His face was white and his eyes were worried. Daniel was digging in his pocket for change to make a phone call while Addie kneeled to comfort Evan.

"Where else could he be?" Jacob worried. He watched Daniel take a quarter from the handful of change he had pulled from his pocket. "What do you think you're gonna do?" he asked.

"Call Dad," Daniel answered. "What else?"

"Why?" Jacob sputtered. "If he finds out we've lost Abe, he'll kill me!"

"Why should he kill you?" Daniel said. "I'm the one who was supposed to be watching him."

"That's not how Dad's gonna see it," Jacob insisted. "He'll blame me for not being 'responsible.' Didn't you hear what he said before we left?"

"That's crazy," Daniel said. "Why do you always think Dad's out to get you?"

"Because he is," Jacob muttered.

"What difference does it make whose fault it is?" Christopher said. "Abe's gone."

Evan began to cry when he heard the tremor in Christopher's voice. Addie hugged the little boy once more. "Let's pray and ask God to help us find him, okay?"

Evan nodded between sniffles and Addie prayed quickly and fervently. "Lord, please help us think. Please show us where Abe is. Thank You. In Jesus' name. Amen." Addie stood up and saw Joanna walking toward them with a smile on her face.

"Are you ready to look for . . . What's the problem?" she asked quickly. "You all look scared to death."

"Our cousin is missing," Jacob said tersely. "He's four years old and we can't find him anywhere."

"Let's tell the head librarian," Joanna said. "She can page him over the intercom."

The children followed her to the desk in the center of the room. Addie had to carry Evan when the little boy began to cry in earnest. He buried his head in her shoulder and sobbed quietly while they listened to the tinny voice of the librarian carry through the library amid a loud crackle of static.

"Would Abraham McCormick please come to the information center on the first floor? Abraham McCormick, please come to the information center. Thank you."

"The first floor?" Jacob said suddenly. "Is there a second floor?"

Joanna shook her head. "No," she said. "Just the basement."

"The basement!" Addie, Jake, and Danny all thought the same thing at the same time and Addie voiced their thoughts.

"He went downstairs to look for me and Jake!"

"'Course he did," Christopher said with obvious relief and some disgust. "The little twerp."

"Did we find him?" Evan's head popped up from Addie's shoulder and he rubbed his eyes, red from tears.

"Not yet," she said, "but we're on the right track."

She set Evan down and they all clattered down the stairs. Abe was nowhere in sight, but they could hear voices at the back of the room. Then Abe's cheerful giggle floated down one of the aisles and they all let out a collective sigh of relief.

"Abraham!" Evan shouted at the top of his voice and Christopher clapped a hand over his mouth.

The door to the storage area opened silently and Abe's solemn face peered out. His eyes were round with fear. He knew he was in trouble.

Christopher began to march down the aisle toward his little brother. "Abe, get out here right *now!*" he called in a loud, hoarse whisper.

Abe's face disappeared and the door clicked shut behind him.

"You little twerp," Christopher muttered and tried the doorknob. It was locked.

"I've got a key," Joanna said, barely able to keep the laughter out of her voice.

But the door opened once more and the elderly janitor appeared, leading a reluctant Abraham by the hand. Abe tried to hide behind his legs while Christopher grabbed roughly at his brother's arm.

"Here, here," the janitor said firmly as he separated the two boys.

"Wait till we get home," Christopher snapped. "Mom finds out you sneaked off to the basement without us, you're gonna be sitting on a chair for the rest of your *life*!" He punched Abe's arm for emphasis and Abe punched back and missed.

"Am not!" the little boy shouted.

"Are too!"

"Cut it out." Jacob pulled them apart this time. "Why didn't you tell us you were down here, Abe?"

Abe shrugged. "You were busy and I saw Ernie carrying a big box and I wanted to know what was in it, so I asked him and he told me and I—"

"Okay, okay," Daniel interrupted. "Let's just tell Ernie thanks so we can call Gram's and go home. I've had my fill of the library for today."

"Thanks, Ernie," Abe said with a shy smile at his new friend.

"You're welcome, Abraham," Ernie replied. "I hope you find your treasure."

"Did you find it, Addie?" Abe asked.

"Addie?" Ernie the janitor studied the young girl carefully. "Are you all Addie McCormick's grandchildren?"

"No," Abe giggled. "She's not our grandma. Gram's our grandma."

Addie grinned at her cousin. "That's who he means, Abe. Gram's name is Addie, too."

"That's dumb," Abe said bluntly, and everyone laughed.

"I didn't know the McCormicks had a 'treasure' in their family," Ernie said in a teasing voice.

Jake grinned. "Neither did we until this week," he said. "No one seems to know what it is or where it's at."

Addie tried to explain their situation as succinctly as possible. "Gram gave me some things that had been given to her by *her* grandmother and it all points to this treasure that someone gave the first Addie back before the Civil War."

Ernie was rubbing his chin thoughtfully. "You want to find out anything about anybody in this town, you ought to talk to Irlene Campbell. Irlene's 98 years old, but she's got a memory like an elephant. About the old days, that is. Can't remember what she had for lunch, of course, but that's the way it is with old folks."

"What'd you have for lunch, Ernie?" Abe asked, and Ernie burst into laughter.

"You think I'm old, Abe?" he chuckled. "I guess you're right, 'cause offhand, I can't remember." He opened the door to the storage room and gave the children a wink. "You talk to Irlene, you want to know anything," he repeated and closed the door behind him, still chuckling.

Joanna offered once more to help them find information on shipwrecks from 1858, but by now everyone was tired. Addie and the older boys decided it was best if they went home.

"Maybe we'll be back tomorrow. Thanks for your help," she told the woman.

Addie's father came to pick them up soon after Daniel made the necessary phone call. When they got back to Gram's, Addie and Jake went straight to the kitchen. Gram and the other women were fixing chili and cornbread for supper. Uncle Lee and Uncle Jim were setting the table in the dining room.

"Mmm, that smells good," Addie said, rubbing her hands together to warm them up. "It's so cold outside."

"Say, Gram, do you know a woman named Irlene Campbell?" Jake asked.

Gram smiled. "Oh, my yes," she said. "Did you meet Irlene at the library?"

"No," Addie told her. "A man there suggested we talk to her if we wanted to know 'anything about anybody,' he said."

"Well, he'd be right," Gram agreed, nodding. "Irlene is just about the oldest woman in town, as far as I know. I haven't seen her myself for quite some time, but from what I hear, she's still going strong. She always made it her business to keep up on the latest gossip."

Abe and Evan joined them in the kitchen and Abe climbed up on Addie's lap. He tried to sneak a cookie from the cookie jar, but his mother intercepted it and set the jar on top of the refrigerator.

Gram gave the children a curious glance. "Who told you about Irlene?"

"Ernie did," Abe said. "He's the janitor."

"How did you manage to drag the janitor into this?" Aunt Bev laughed.

Abe shrugged. "I just met him and he told us," he said and avoided his mother's glance. Aunt Bev knew her middle son well enough to know when she was being sidetracked.

"Abe," she said in a knowing voice. "What happened?"

Abe's little chest heaved a gigantic sigh and he looked at Addie and Jake. Addie told them the story of Abe's brief disappearance and Aunt Bev frowned at the little boy.

"That's going to earn you a time-out on the chair," she said and pointed to the dining room.

"How long?" Abe asked in a dejected voice.

"Ten minutes," Aunt Bev said firmly.

Abe's face brightened considerably. Ten minutes was a far cry from "the rest of your life." The little boy trotted, almost happily, into the dining room and hopped onto the chair that always sat in the corner when Aunt Bev and Uncle Jim were visiting. Aunt Bev watched him with a puzzled expression, then simply shrugged and shook her head.

Uncle Lee had been listening from the dining room door. Now he entered the kitchen. "Just where were you when all this happened?" he asked Jake.

Jake frowned and Addie could see his whole body stiffen. "Addie and I were downstairs looking for the—"

"I thought I told you that you had to be responsible for those kids!"

"Daniel was supposed to be watching—"

"Don't blame your brother! We agreed you weren't going to make him do all the work!"

"I didn't!" Jacob shouted the words and he pushed back his chair with a loud scrape.

"Where do you think you're going?" his father asked.

"To my room," Jacob snapped.

"Good. Stay there until I tell you differently."

Jacob stared at his father for a long moment, then stormed past him and headed for the stairs.

Daniel passed Jake in the dining room and tried to stop him, but Jake pulled out of his grasp and ran up the stairs two at a time.

Daniel came in the kitchen and looked at his father with troubled eyes. "Dad, it was my fault Abe got lost today. Jake watched the kids first, for almost an hour. I went upstairs to relieve him and Evan and I started working on a puzzle. Before I knew it, Abe was gone."

Uncle Lee stared at his oldest son and all the anger seemed to drain from his body. No one spoke. Above them, a door slammed shut with such force that the cups in Gram's cupboard rattled gently.

CHAPTER 9

Irlene

Uncle Lee and Jacob spent the next half hour behind Jacob's closed door while the rest of the family ate a very quiet supper. When the two finally came downstairs, Jacob took his customary seat next to Addie, but he didn't say anything. Down the table, Addie could hear her uncle's deep voice make an occasional comment, but he was unusually quiet as well.

Jacob didn't finish his bowl of chili and left his cornbread untouched. He excused himself from the table and went back upstairs. He stayed there for the rest of the evening. Addie and Daniel went to the living room and played a game of two-handed spades while the younger boys all watched a Disney movie they had rented from the local video store.

"So what's your next step in looking for the treasure?" Daniel asked. He trumped her jack of diamonds with a spade and Addie frowned. She had a handful of diamonds.

"I'm not sure." Addie sighed. She wished Jake was there to help her think. "We're not having much luck finding out about the ship that Harrison Haile was on. Maybe we should concentrate on the fire. That's when the treasure disappeared."

"I bet Irlene Campbell would know about that fire," Daniel observed.

Gram was rocking baby Lindsey, making soft noises and kissing the little girl's fingers. When she heard Daniel mention Irlene Campbell's name, she looked up.

"I could call Irlene in the morning if you want to talk to her," Gram said. "I'm sure there's a lot she could tell you, and I know she'd love the company."

"Okay," Addie nodded. "I hope—" She wasn't sure how to finish the sentence tactfully, so Daniel did it for her.

"You hope Jacob wants to go along. He will. He'll get over his bad mood and be okay in the morning. That's what usually happens."

Daniel hesitated on the "usually" and gave Addie a troubled glance. He lowered his voice. "You know, he's always bellyached about the way Dad picks on him. I never believed it. I guess I just thought he was jealous of me."

Daniel paused and Addie studied her cards, careful to avoid his gaze. "Do you think Dad treats him differently than he does me?"

Addie sighed and chose her words carefully. "I think your dad understands you better than he understands Jake."

"That's for sure," Daniel said. "I don't know anybody who understands Jake—except you."

Addie didn't answer and Daniel shifted uncomfortably. "I didn't mean that as an insult," he said.

"I know," she smiled. "I don't understand Jake myself sometimes, but I always have fun with him. He makes me think. I look at things differently when I'm with him."

"He's pretty smart," Daniel agreed. "I always thought it would be fun to know how to take things apart and put them back together like he does. It just makes Dad mad when he does that." Daniel shook his head and sat quietly for several long moments.

Addie stretched and yawned, and Daniel grinned. "Am I keeping you up?" he teased.

Addie grinned. "I think I could fall asleep right here."

Daniel nodded. "Maybe I'll hit the sack early myself. I'll go see what Jake's up to." He trumped Addie's highest club and she threw down her cards in disgust.

"You win," she said.

"As usual," Daniel said with a smirk. He added his cards to the pile and stood up. "Night, Addie. Night, Gram."

"Good night, dear," Gram said and Addie gave a wave of her hand.

"Where's Danny going?" Abe looked up from his movie and watched his oldest cousin run lightly up the stairs.

"To bed," Gram said.

Abe was aghast. "We *never* go to bed early at your house, Gram."

"I think he wants to spend some time with Jake," Gram said. She smiled warmly at Addie. "Thanks to you, dear. You handled that very well."

Addie colored slightly at Gram's compliment. "I just hope I helped. I wish other people could see Jake the way I do. Especially his dad."

Gram sighed. "History repeating itself," she said.

"What?" Addie was confused.

"Didn't you ever notice who got along with Jake better than anyone?" Gram asked.

Addie's eyes widened. "Grandpa."

Gram nodded. "He taught Jake everything he knew about taking things apart. And Grandpa could never understand why Uncle Lee had more interest in football than he did in mechanical things."

Addie tried to take in everything Gram was telling her. So Grandpa never understood his own son, Uncle Lee. And now Uncle Lee was just as perplexed by Jake. Addie shook her head, trying to untangle the complicated threads of family relationships.

Later that night, when her parents came to pray with her, she had a question for her father.

"Did you get along with Grandpa?" she asked her father bluntly.

He seemed surprised by the question, but only for a second. "Dad and I got along great," he smiled. "Denny and Jim were close to him, too. But Lee . . . well, he and Lee clashed sometimes."

Addie's mom raised one eyebrow and her father grimaced. "Okay, they clashed a lot. It helps you understand the problems Jake and Uncle Lee have, doesn't it?"

Addie nodded.

"It doesn't make it right," her dad continued. "I think there were things Dad and Lee could have done to get along better. And I know there are ways Jake and Lee could be closer. But they both need to compromise."

Addie nodded again. "Has anyone told them that?" she asked.

Her father laughed. "Maybe that's what the Lord wants you to do," he said.

* * *

Addie and the younger boys were already eating breakfast when Jake and Danny came downstairs Friday morning. They were talking quietly and Jake gave Addie a slight smile when they entered the room.

"Daniel said we're going to talk to that old lady today," he said. He made no mention of the previous night's problems.

Addie wrinkled her nose at him. "Don't call her an old lady, Jake. Call her Mrs. Campbell."

Jake smiled sheepishly. "Sorry. I don't think about how I sound sometimes. Has Gram called her yet?"

"Yes, I have." Gram answered his question from the stove, where she was stirring oatmeal. "I'm not sure she understood what we're looking for, but I decided it would be easier if you told her in person. She's looking forward to your visit. I think she might even try to bake cookies before you get there."

"I love cookies," Abe declared and the four older children all looked at one another in dismay.

Aunt Bev spoke before any of them could voice their thoughts. "You're going to stay home this morning, my dear. I'm afraid that's part of your punishment for your little escapade yesterday."

Abe's bottom lip protruded once more, but Aunt Bev ignored it. "You're done with breakfast, so why don't you take Evan to the living room and play with Legos?"

Abe climbed down from his chair without a word and took his little brother by the hand. He walked silently from the room, staring woefully over his shoulder all the way out.

"What an actor," Aunt Bev muttered and the other children laughed.

"Who's taking us to Mrs. Campbell's house?" Daniel asked.

"Why don't you walk?" Gram suggested. "It's warmed up some and the walk will do you good."

The idea appealed to the children, and soon they were bundled up and racing one another down Gram's hill. Christopher was surprisingly fast for his age and took Addie and Jake by surprise. Daniel won easily but it was a close race for second place. Jake inched ahead at the last minute with Chris and Addie tying for third.

Their impromptu run winded them all and no one said much until they passed the library.

"Gram said it was a block south of the library. A big yellow house on the corner," Addie said.

"There it is." Christopher saw the house first and he crossed the street and ran up the front steps. Addie, Jake, and Daniel were right behind him.

The yellow paint had faded over the years and it was badly chipped in some places. There was a crack in the window of the front door and the screen was popped out at the top.

"Place could use some work," Jake said critically. He pounded on the door as loud as he could.

"Give her a break, would you?" Daniel frowned at his brother. "She is 98 years old."

The woman who answered the door surprised them all. She was tall, almost as tall as Gram, with thin gray hair cropped close to her head. Her eyes were dark brown and looked larger than normal behind her thick bifocal glasses. She walked slowly, with a cane, but there was nothing about her that even hinted at frailty or extreme old age. She opened the door and beckoned them inside without a word.

Addie swallowed and spoke first. "Hi, Mrs. Campbell, we're—"

"I know who you are," Irlene interrupted her. "You hungry?"

None of them were, but none of them had the nerve to refuse the plateful of cookies she picked up from the coffee table. After distributing coconut macaroons, she set the plate down and peered at Addie over the top of her glasses.

"So you're another Adlon, eh?" she asked briskly. "Too many Adlons in that family. Very confusing. Didn't help much when they threw in a Nolda and a Londa. 'Course, I could keep 'em straight, but no one else ever knew who was who."

"Gram said you might know something about the fire our family had a long time ago," Addie told her.

"'Course I know about that fire," Mrs. Campbell said. "That's all Nolda talked about—that and her dead husband."

"Did you know Granny Nolda?" Jake asked.

"Yep. Her daughter Adlon—not your Gram, but the Adlon before *her*—we were friends. Born the same year, 1895. I spent lots of time with her and Nolda. Tried their best to convert me. Always preaching at me about the love of Jesus."

The children exchanged knowing grins, but Mrs. Campbell didn't notice.

"Never took much to religion myself. Gotta admit, though, it saw Nolda through some hard times. Nolda's husband drowned when me and Addie were just teenagers. Nolda set to work and raised them kids by herself. She never saw it that way, 'course. Always said Spirit of God was guiding her hand and the grace of God covered her mistakes."

"You said she talked a lot about the fire," Addie prompted her gently.

"Oh, yes," Mrs. Campbell said. "'Course, that fire was before my day. Nolda was engaged to be married when her folks' house burned. Her whole trousseau went up in smoke. She liked to brag to me and Addie about all the little trinkets and geegaws she collected before the wedding. Then she'd say, 'But it all burned when the house burned. Only the grace of God I got anything left.'"

Irlene shook her head in disbelief. "I couldn't never understand the grace of God that would burn down your house and drown your husband."

"God didn't do those things!" The words burst out before Addie could stop them, and Irlene peered at the young girl with a knowing smile.

"Yep. You're one of the family, all right. Nolda never once pointed a finger at God. Kinda admired her for that."

"Um, she did say that she had something left from the fire, though. Right?" Jacob frowned at Addie and tried to get Mrs. Campbell back on track.

Irlene nodded. "Addie's inheritance, for one thing."

"You know about that?" Addie gasped.

"Whole town knew about that! Nolda was as proud of those little geegaws as a body could be. There was a necklace of some sort and a pichure and there was the gold, 'course. No one else in town had gold miners for grandparents."

Christopher interrupted her. "Was it a lot of gold?"

"'Course not. As I understood it, most of the gold was lost when her grandparents came back from prospectin' in California. The ship they was on went down in a hurricane. The wife was rescued, but the husband drowned. All the wife had was some nuggets tucked in her corset."

"Winnie and Harrison Haile," Addie said softly.

Irlene nodded. "That's the folks."

"Do you know the name of the ship?" Daniel asked.

Irlene shook her head. "Nope. But that's engraved on her tombstone, as I recall. Your family's always been one for writing on the tombstones."

"Where's the gold now?" Jake wanted to know.

"That I couldn't tell you for sure." Irlene shrugged. "Nolda could be pretty close about certain things. Didn't want to keep her valuables at home. Always afraid of another fire. So she left 'em with a friend. Everyone always suspected it was Mary, but Nolda wouldn't say."

"Who was Mary?" Daniel asked.

"Mary Brockworth, her best friend."

Addie took a deep breath and gave Jake a triumphant grin. The pieces to the puzzle were finally falling in place.

CHAPTER 10

Addie Weston

The walk home passed quickly. The children were so excited, none of them noticed the cold or the wind or the gray clouds on the horizon. They made the trip up Gram's long hill almost as quickly as they had come down. Despite the cold, Addie was hot when she burst through the front door, and she dropped her coat in the front entry.

"Gram," she shouted, heading for the kitchen. Aunt Jenny intercepted the four children in the dining room with a finger to her lips.

"Aunt Bev just got Lindsey to sleep," she whispered. "Keep the noise down." She smiled at the flushed cheeks and covered her ears at the barrage of excited whispers as the children crowded around her, anxious to tell someone their good fortune.

"Come in the kitchen, we'll shut the door, and everyone can hear what you have to say," she laughed.

It took some minutes for the children to calm down and agree to let Addie be their spokesman. By that time everyone in the family had heard there was exciting news and they all crowded around the large kitchen table or sat on Gram's counters.

"Winnie *and* Harrison Haile went to California prospecting for gold," Addie began. "They came back on a ship that went down in a hurricane. Mrs. Campbell couldn't remember the name of the ship, but she said it was engraved on Winnie's tombstone."

"So all we have to do is find that tombstone if we want to know the name of the ship," Jake put in.

"Harrison Haile drowned," Addie continued, "but Winnie was saved. Most of their gold was lost, except for what Winnie had tucked in her corset." All the adults laughed at that news.

"What's a corset, anyway?" Christopher asked Gram.

"Or a 'geegaw' or a 'tru-so'?" Daniel mimicked Irlene Campbell's rough voice.

Gram laughed heartily. "I can see Irlene is still quite a character," she said. "Well, a corset is something like a girdle." Chris made a face.

"A geegaw is just another word for a trinket, and a trousseau is all the things a girl saves to take to her new home when she gets married," Jake finished for her.

"Right," Gram nodded. Her eyes sparkled. "So there really is gold involved."

Addie nodded. "But that's not all," she told her audience. "Irlene said there was a necklace of some sort and a pitcher, too."

Jake laughed. "Now you're starting to talk like Irlene," he teased his cousin.

"What?"

"It's a pic-ture," he said, sounding out the syllables, "not a pichure."

Addie shook her head. "I thought she meant a pitcher, like a milk pitcher."

Gram smiled. "That is confusing," she said. "But I think Jake is probably right. Granny Nolda had a very nice photo album. Did you see it when you were in the attic the other night?"

Addie nodded. "Probably. I saw several. I thought they were yours."

"Most of them are. Some are my mother's. It probably wouldn't hurt to look at them, especially Granny Nolda's," Gram said. "There might be some information there." She sighed. "I've been meaning to sort through those and have some of the older pictures restored. Maybe I'll do that soon."

"Addie," Christopher whispered, "don't forget about that Mary lady."

"Mary who?" Gram asked.

"Mary Brockworth was Granny Nolda's best friend. Irlene thinks Granny Nolda probably asked Mary to store the few valuables she saved from the fire. She was always afraid of having another fire."

"What if Mary's house burned down?" Abraham asked wisely. The little boy had listened intently to all that had been said.

Addie looked momentarily distressed. "Good question, Abe. I hope it didn't."

Gram was still puzzled. "The name Mary Brockworth doesn't ring a bell with me. I don't recall any Brockworths in Camp Point."

Uncle Lee had the phone book out and was looking through the *B*'s.

He shook his head. "There aren't any Brockworths here anymore," he said.

That was a disappointment, but Addie wasn't discouraged for long. "There's got to be someone who remembers her. If nothing else, we can go back to Irlene and find out what happened to her."

"I want to go to the cemetery and look for Winnie Haile's tombstone," Jacob said.

But Gram was shaking her head again. "Winnie Haile isn't in the family plot," she said. "I take flowers there twice a year and I've never seen a tombstone with her name. It could be in the old cemetery," she mused. "But that's been fenced off and locked up for years. The Historical Society keeps saying they're going to clean it up and open it again, but they never have."

She snapped her fingers. "Uncle Ed. If anyone can get you in the old cemetery, it's Ed. He might even know who Mary Brockworth was." She reached for the phone as she spoke and dialed Ed's number before the words were out of her mouth.

Addie jumped down from the stool she was sitting on. "How much time before lunch?" she asked.

"Only an hour," her mother smiled. "Not enough time to go prowling through graveyards."

"Let's look at those photo albums," Addie said to her cousins. "I know right where they are in the attic."

"I love attics," Abe said with a timid smile.

Addie laughed. "Sure, Abe. You and Evan can come with us. I don't think Gram will care if we all snoop around her attic before lunch."

Gram was still on the phone with Uncle Ed, but she heard the exchange and gave them permission with a wink and a nod.

Christopher led the charge up to the attic. Addie, Abe, and Evan lagged behind. The older boys were all peering into dusty cartons when she and the little ones arrived. Addie went straight to the boxes where she'd seen the photo albums the first night.

The albums on top belonged to Gram. Addie and her cousins spent most of their time skimming through pictures of their parents' early years. It was funny to see their fathers at the same ages they were now. Addie's father wore black-rimmed glasses and had very skinny legs. Uncle Jim once had a headfull of black hair and Uncle Denny wasn't always so tall and strong.

But the pictures of Uncle Lee interested Addie the most. In most of the family photos Uncle Lee was outside the warm circle of activity. His smile was often strained and his eyes were more often trained on his father than on the camera.

Jake's gaze seemed to linger on those photos, and he looked up to see Addie staring at him. He blushed and turned the page quickly.

"There's nothing in Gram's albums," Jake muttered. "Let's look at the others."

Daniel picked up one that belonged to Gram's mother. The pictures in it were much older, but they were able to recognize Gram as a little girl. She looked remarkably like Addie. Years passed and Gram grew up quickly. Then came pictures of Uncle Ed and his army buddy, Ken McCormick. Soon Uncle Ed disappeared from the pictures and Gram took his place next to the soldier. Her marriage to Grandpa followed and the last page of the album held two pictures. One showed Gram standing in a doorway with a newborn baby—Addie's father. The second showed Gram, Grandpa, John as a toddler, and Lee as the newborn in Gram's arms.

"We're never going to get to Granny Nolda's album if we look at all the pictures," Daniel said. "Let's skip the rest of these."

Addie agreed. She dug down through the box and found the album they were looking for. It was heavy, black, and very plain. It didn't zip or have a padded cover like the others. The photos inside were different as well. These pictures were printed on much heavier paper, almost like cardboard. The faces were all very solemn—no spontaneous smiles or goofy faces here. These people had obviously posed for their portraits.

Evan wrinkled his nose at the strange-looking photographs. "Where's the happy people?" he asked.

Jake laughed. "These people were probably happy, Evan. But they usually didn't smile for the camera. If they moved at all, it blurred the picture."

Of course, the children didn't recognize any of these faces and there weren't any names to identify them. Daniel was soon discouraged.

"What are we looking for, anyway?" he asked.

Addie just shrugged. "I'm not sure."

"If we don't know what we're looking for, how will we know when we find it?" Abe asked sensibly.

Addie smiled in spite of herself. "For a four-year-old kid, you ask some pretty smart questions," was her only answer.

She turned the last page of the album and gave a low whistle. "Maybe this is it," she murmured.

A large, yellowed envelope was tucked in the back of the album. Inside were several more pictures. They were tintypes, very old pictures printed on thin iron. Addie lifted them carefully from the envelope.

There were six tintypes in all. A young, petite woman was in all of them and Addie checked the back to see if there were names given. "W. Haile" was scratched on the back of the first one.

"This is Winnie Haile," she said excitedly. The second was a picture of Winnie and a little girl, about two years old. They were seated on a high-backed chair, wearing dark dresses and bonnets. The next two pictures were similar poses of mother and daughter as the little girl grew older.

Addie stared, fascinated by the first "Addie" in her family. The little girl had a thin face and large, dark eyes that seemed old for her years. Addie hardly noticed when Jake took the last two tintypes from her hands.

"Addie. Addie!" Jake's urgent whisper jarred Addie from her reverie. "Look at this one."

The tintype Jake was holding showed two young women, Winnie Haile and a friend, standing in front of a large brick building. Although they were the focus of the picture, hundreds of people streamed down a sidewalk to their left. Winnie held the baby Addie in her arms. On the back of the tintype, someone had scratched in three names—W. Haile, A. Haile and A. Weston. Underneath the names was another word that looked like Chicago, except the *ic* was missing. Underneath *that* was a sentence, but it wasn't legible. It was close to the bottom of the tin and years of handling had worn off most of the letters.

"This is the original Addie," Jake said to his cousins. Everyone gathered around to see the legendary woman. "Remember the letter? It was signed Addie W. That's her. Addie Weston."

"And the other woman is Winnie Haile, with her baby Addie." Addie took the tintype back from Jake and turned it over once more. "I wish we could read what this bottom line says!"

She held it up to study it by the light of the window behind her. "That first word starts with an L. Then there's an *i* and maybe that's an *o*, and there's an *n*."

"I can't make out hardly any of the letters in the second word. Just another *i* and an *n* again," said Jake.

"That word is *the*," Christopher said and pointed to the third word.

Daniel nodded. "You're right, Chris. The next word ends in *rst* and the last word looks like *picture*."

The children all studied the cryptic message, but nothing they came up with made any sense.

"If you just read the letters you can see, it says there's a lion in the picture," Christopher said.

"Let's show this to Gram," Addie said. "I don't think she knew this was here. Maybe she can figure it out. Where'd Abe and Evan go now?"

The two little boys had wandered to the far end of the attic. They were sitting in an empty box they had tipped over on its side. Chris herded them out and the group went back to the kitchen.

Gram was making ham sandwiches at the counter. She couldn't read the message either, but she was thrilled with their discovery. "So Addie Weston was her name. I never knew that. I've never even seen this picture before. This is wonderful! I'm going to have this reprinted and enlarged.

"And," she beamed at the children, "Uncle Ed knows the president of the Historical Society. He's going to get a key and take you to the old cemetery after lunch. You're going to find this treasure yet!"

CHAPTER 11

The Crown Jewel

Gram went back to making ham sandwiches and the children sat down around the table to wait for lunch.

"I wonder where this cemetery is?" Daniel asked.

"I love cemeteries," Abe announced.

Jake grinned at the little boy. "What don't you love?"

"Abe," Chris said impatiently, "cemeteries are where they bury people."

Abe looked concerned. "*Real* people?"

Chris leaned over, grabbed Abe's arm, and whispered in his brother's ear. "Yeah. Real *dead* ones."

Fortunately for Chris, none of the adults heard this exchange. Abe's eyes grew large and he pulled hastily out of his brother's grasp. He jumped off his chair to run from the room and bumped into his father.

"I'm not goin' to no cemetery," he said, and poked his father's leg for emphasis. "I'm staying right here. Come on, Evan."

Evan trotted obediently after his brother and Uncle Jim watched them go with a quizzical look on his face.

"You guys going to the cemetery?" he asked the older kids.

"Uncle Ed's taking us to find Winnie Haile's grave," Addie explained.

"I don't think Abe wants to go," Chris said.

"No kidding. When's lunch?"

"As soon as someone sets the table." Gram set two big platters of sandwiches in front of Daniel. "No one eats until everything's ready."

The older children, famished from their walk to Irlene's, all scrambled for plates, silverware, glasses, and napkins. The table was ready in short order, the family gathered, and Gram blessed the food.

Uncle Ed knocked on the back door just as lunch was winding down. He grabbed a sandwich while the children donned coats and hats.

"Bundle up good," he told them. "The wind's picked up and it's beginning to snow. I think we're in for a storm."

Everyone headed for the car, but Addie hesitated. "I'll be right there," she told them. She ran to the study and found a tablet of drawing paper in Gram's desk and took a sheet. She rolled it up and tucked it inside her coat, along with a heavy lead pencil. Then she took the letter and key from her box. She folded the key carefully inside the letter and put them both in the inside zippered pocket on the other side of her coat. Then she ran out to the car.

Addie and Jake sat in front this time, while Chris and Danny took the backseat. Uncle Ed turned left at the bottom of Gram's hill and headed out of town.

"The old cemetery is only about a mile away," he said. "But it's set back a ways and the lane is hard to see. Help me watch for it. It'll be on your left."

They all peered out their windows, and it was Chris who spied the narrow dirt road, hidden by dry brown weeds and brush. Uncle Ed turned down the lane and drove up and over a small hill.

Behind the hill was a high iron fence, rusty and in need of repair. They parked the car and Uncle Ed led them to the gate that was locked with a simple chain and padlock. He opened it with a small key and the gate swung back with a reluctant groan.

The cemetery was small. The children could see from one end to the other and from side to side. Most of the tombstones were cracked and weathered, overgrown with dead weeds and bushes. The engravings on many of the stones had been worn smooth by the elements. Standing there in the open, the wind was fierce and everyone was shivering.

"Well, it shouldn't take long to find her if she's here," Uncle Ed said. "Why don't we split up and take rows? We'll work from end to end, rather than side to side."

Everyone agreed and it didn't take long for them to work their way through the cemetery. Most of the names were still legible and the children moved quickly in the bitter wind. It was Chris, again, who found what they were looking for.

"Here she is! Here she is!" he called, jumping up and down with excitement and cold. Everyone ran to join him, and Addie and Jake read the inscription on the stone in unison.

Here Lies Winifred Johnson Haile
Born 1840 Died 1895
Faithful Wife of Harrison,
Loving Mother of Adlon
The Sacred Bonds of Matrimony
Tragically Severed Years Earlier
by the Sinking of the Crown Jewel.
The Lord Giveth and the Lord Taketh Away.
Blessed Be the Name of the Lord.

"The *Crown Jewel*," Jake repeated. "That should be easy to find."

Addie was looking around her at the other tombstones and Uncle Ed smiled. He beckoned to her and she followed him to a smaller stone several rows over.

"She's buried here with her husband in his family plot," he said and pointed to the grave of Adlon Haile Kelley. Her inscription was similar.

Here Lies Adlon Haile Kelley
Born 1859 Died 1912
Wife of Randolph,
Mother of Nolda, Joseph, William, and Edward
When Thou Saidst, "Seek Ye My Face,"
My Heart Said Unto Thee,
"Thy Face Lord Will I Seek."

Addie took the drawing paper and pencil from her coat pocket. The paper wasn't large enough to get the whole name, so Addie made a rubbing of "Adlon Haile" and her date of birth and date of death.

Jake came over to see what she was doing. "Pretty cool," he said when he saw the rubbing. "Ready to go?"

Addie shivered. "You bet."

Uncle Ed locked the iron gate and they left the little cemetery. When they reached the bottom of Gram's hill, Uncle Ed stopped.

"Do you want to go home? Or is there somewhere else I can take you?"

"I think we should go back to see Irlene," Addie said. Uncle Ed had not recognized the name Mary Brockworth, so it appeared Mrs. Campbell was their only lead to the mysterious woman.

"And I want to go to the library and find the news reports about the sinking of the *Crown Jewel*," Jake added.

"Are you going to be using that machine again?" Christopher asked.

Jake nodded and the boy sighed.

"You can go home with Uncle Ed," Addie told her cousin. "Jake and Daniel and I can—"

"Uh, I was hoping to get back and watch the ball game on television this afternoon," Daniel put in.

So Uncle Ed dropped Addie and Jake off in front of Irlene Campbell's house. "Call when you're ready to leave," he shouted over the howl of the wind. It was blowing hard now and snow was swirling lightly all around them. "You don't want to walk home in this!"

Addie nodded and waved as Uncle Ed pulled away. She and Jake ran up Irlene's front steps. They pounded hard on her front door and peered in the window for some sign of the elderly woman. But she didn't appear, so Jake pounded louder and they rubbed their arms and stomped their feet to ward off the cold as they waited. After several minutes, they gave up and ran down the street to the library.

The air inside felt uncommonly warm, but it was a relief to the two freezing children. They headed straight for the basement and found Joanna at her desk. She smiled broadly when she saw them.

"The name of the ship was the *Crown Jewel*," Jake said without any preliminaries.

"Great!" Joanna exclaimed. She held up two large books she had to one side of her desk. One was titled *America's History of Tragedy at Sea*. The other was *Treasure Hunting: Bounties of the Sea*. She handed the first to Addie and Jake and thumbed through the index of the second one herself.

"Here it is," Addie murmured. The sinking of the *Crown Jewel* was described in some detail in a chapter titled, "Gold at the Bottom of the Sea." The ship had gone down in a hurricane on September 27, 1858. The details given included the amount of gold believed to be on board, the number of passengers who had died, the valiant attempts at rescue by smaller ships passing in the fierce gale, and the many medals posthumously bestowed on the captain, who had gone down with his ship.

Joanna's book told little else, but hers had a footnote at the bottom of the page. "This says, 'For further reference, please see *Heroism at Sea: The Sinking of the Crown Jewel*.' I'll run upstairs and check the main computer to see if we have it in circulation."

"Can we go back to the microfilm and see if you have any issues dated on or around September 27, 1858?" Jake asked.

"Of course," Joanna said. She went to the cabinet and pulled out a canister with the dates January 1858–December 1858. "If we've got copies of those papers, they'd be on this reel."

Addie and Jake were experienced with the microfilm machine by now, so Joanna left them to their work and disappeared up the steps.

It was a very disappointing search. There were no copies of any papers between September 4, 1858, and November 1, 1858. The sinking of the ship was still news at the beginning of November, but the articles were limited to personal accounts by survivors, though none by Winnie Haile, and editorials that praised the virtues of the esteemed captain of the doomed vessel.

Addie flicked the off button of the machine just as Joanna appeared at their side. In her hand she held a copy of the book *Heroism at Sea: The Sinking of the Crown Jewel*. Her finger marked a spot in the book, and she opened it up and set it on the table in front of Addie and Jake. Her eyes sparkled as she pointed to a very old black-and-white picture.

"Is this what you've been looking for?" she asked.

It was the picture of Winnie Haile and her baby Addie standing next to Adlon Weston.

CHAPTER 12

The Storm

"How did you find this?" Addie exclaimed.

Joanna smiled. "I remembered your grandmother's name. There's a list of survivors at the beginning of the book. They each wrote a personal account of the tragedy. This is Winnie's. It's quite a story."

Addie pushed the book closer to Jake so they could both read it. It was indeed quite a story. Winnie and Harrison Haile had been married only a few short months when they decided to head west and prospect for gold. To their surprise, good fortune came quickly and in large measure. They intended to stay longer in California, but Winnie became pregnant with their first child and the decision was made to return to Harrison's home in Connecticut so their child could be born and raised among family.

The trip home was an arduous one. Because Winnie was five months pregnant and in poor health, they chose the relative safety and comfort of passage on a steamship. On the voyage from California, Winnie and Harrison became good friends with another young married couple, Addie and Arden Weston, who had also been west and found gold. It was Addie who kept the young mother-to-be company during her worst bouts of morning sickness and fatigue.

The first leg of their voyage was aboard the steamship *Minerva*. When they arrived in Panama, the passengers left the *Minerva* and boarded the Panama Railroad for the short trip to the Atlantic coast. There they were transferred to the ill-fated *Crown Jewel*.

Two days into their trip, the *Crown Jewel* entered the fringes of a hurricane. The ship was battered by high winds and waves for several hours. Many became seasick, including Adlon Weston. Strangely enough, the weather did not affect Winnie, and she was able to spend the time with her "dear friend Addie, offering her just a pittance of the comfort she had given me at my bedside."

That evening, a leak was discovered and the ship began to take on water. During the night, the rising water extinguished the boilers and the ship was adrift at sea. Bailing did no good, and it became apparent the ship was doomed. When another ship was sighted at dawn, women and children were lowered into lifeboats to await rescue. Because of her condition, Winnie was one of the first women to be evacuated and Addie Weston accompanied her, although their husbands remained aboard. The next paragraph brought tears to Addie's eyes.

> Our time of separation drew nearer, as
> the lifeboats were lowered; yet I sat close
> to my beloved Harrison and we talked of
> our hopes, our plans for the future, and

> the dreams we had for the child yet to be born. Then we commended ourselves into God's loving care and embraced one last time. Harrison remained calm and at peace to the end. The memory of my husband's steadfast demeanor strengthened my spirit and quieted my tears in the days to come.

Addie swallowed hard and kept reading. All the women and children aboard the *Crown Jewel* were rescued. After the ship sank that morning, 50 more men were rescued from the water by a passing freighter. Arden Weston was among them, but Harrison Haile was lost at sea.

That was the end of Winnie Haile's personal account, but a sidebar next to the picture continued her story. The trauma of her experience at sea had greatly endangered Winnie's pregnancy. By the time the survivors arrived in New York, it was feared she would lose her baby. Instead of traveling on to Harrison's family home in Connecticut, Winnie spent the next four months, bedridden, at the New York home of Addie and Arden Weston. There, on January 28, 1859, her daughter Adlon was born.

After recovering from the birth of her child, Winnie went on to Connecticut to visit her deceased husband's family. She finally arrived home in Wisconsin in May of 1859.

The picture of Winnie, her daughter, and Adlon Weston was taken in Chicago in May of 1860. Winnie and her young daughter traveled there to meet

Addie and Arden, who were on their way west again, hoping to regain the fortune they had lost nearly two years earlier.

Addie sat back and waited for Jake to finish the story.

"Wow," was all he could say, and Addie agreed with a nod.

Joanna had returned to her desk, but when she saw they were finished she came back to their table.

"You can check that book out if you'd like," she said.

"We don't have a card here," Addie reminded her.

"Oh, dear," Joanna replied with a frown. "Tell you what. I'll check it out on my card. That way you can take it home and your grandmother can return it for you next week."

"Thanks," Addie smiled. "You've really been a big help."

Joanna grinned. "That's what librarians live for," she laughed. She glanced at her watch. "We'll have to hurry. The weather has really kicked up and there's a winter storm warning out, so the library is closing earlier than usual tonight," she told them. "Will you need a ride home?"

"That would be great," Addie said. "If it's not too much trouble."

"No trouble at all." Joanna took the book from Addie and hurried upstairs.

Ernie came out of the back room pushing his cart of cleaning supplies. He saw the two children sitting at the desk. They waved and he waved back. He put the cart in the closet and came down the aisle.

"Library's closing soon," he said. "Snowin' real bad out there. You kids got a way home?"

Jake grinned. "Joanna just offered to take us," he told their elderly friend.

"No need for that," Ernie said. "I live just the other side of your grandma's hill, outta town about two miles. I can drop you off on my way home."

Addie and Jake looked at each other and shrugged.

"Let me know," Ernie said. "I've still got a few things to pick up before I leave."

Ernie disappeared into the back room once more. Addie picked up *America's History of Tragedy at Sea* and began reading about the *Titanic*.

Jake reached for *Treasure Hunting: Bounties of the Sea* but changed his mind. "I'm going upstairs to the bathroom," he told Addie.

She nodded absentmindedly, already absorbed in the story of the most famous shipwreck of all time. She read silently for several minutes. Suddenly she realized someone was standing next to her. She looked up, expecting to see Jake. Instead, Ernie was smiling down at her.

"You want that ride?" he asked.

"I don't think so, Ernie," she said. "I've got some questions I'd like to ask Joanna. We'll wait for her. Thanks, anyway." Addie smiled at the kindly old man.

"Suit yourself," he said amiably. "I hope you find what you're looking for. Bye now."

Addie watched him trudge slowly up the basement stairs. Then she went back to her story.

Jake joined her shortly and sat down in his chair. He saw that Addie was still deep in her story, so he began reading himself. Several minutes passed.

Addie finished her chapter on the *Titanic* and closed the book. Jake looked up with a smile.

"Interesting?" he asked.

Addie wrinkled her nose. "Very interesting— but sad."

Jake shrugged. "I've never heard of a happy shipwreck," he said dryly.

Addie laughed. "Yeah, I guess you're right," she said. Then she noticed what he was reading. It was *Heroism at Sea: The Sinking of the Crown Jewel.* "Where'd you get that?" she asked.

"I saw Joanna upstairs," he said. "She gave it to me."

"Where is she now?" Addie asked him.

"I told her Ernie was taking us to Gram's, so she left. It's really getting bad outside. I hope Ernie's ready to go pretty soon." Jake looked toward the back room for some sign of the janitor.

Addie groaned. "Great," she muttered.

"What?"

"I told Ernie that Joanna was taking us home. He left about ten minutes ago."

Jake's mouth dropped open, then he began to laugh. "You mean we had two offers for a ride and now we've got none?"

Addie grinned back. "You got it."

"Oh well," Jake said. "Let's go upstairs and use the phone. Someone from home will come get us."

They hurried up the steps to the first floor and walked into a darkened room.

"Holy smokes," Jake whispered. "The place is deserted!"

"Let's find the lights," Addie whispered back. Then she giggled. "Why are we whispering?"

"Because this is a spooky place when you're all alone," Jake answered in a normal tone. His voice echoed loudly and then got swallowed up in the empty room. "That was weird," he whispered.

They walked slowly and close together across the floor to the information desk. It took forever to reach the platform. When Addie stepped up behind the desk she felt exposed and vulnerable.

"Here's the phone," she murmured and picked up the receiver. The buzz of the dial tone was a reassuring sound and she punched in Gram's number quickly.

The number rang once, twice, and then there was a loud click. It sounded as if someone answered the phone, but she couldn't hear a voice. Then the dial tone came back.

She gave Jake a frantic look and he took the receiver from her. "That's okay, we'll just try again," he said. He punched the number in again. One ring, two rings, click. He tried again. One ring, two rings, three rings, click.

"What's the problem?" he wondered.

"The weather is probably messing up the telephone lines," Addie said.

Jake sat the receiver back on the hook. "You know, one time I tried to call Mom from the school. I couldn't hear her, but she could hear me. Maybe we should try again and just talk as if there's someone listening."

"Anything's worth a try," Addie said.

Jake punched the number in one more time. After two rings and a click, he began talking. "Addie and I are stuck at the library. They closed early and we were left here by mistake. Somebody come get us!"

He stared into the receiver then, as if looking for someone, and Addie giggled. He blushed and hung up.

"What do we do now?" Addie asked.

"Let's go see how bad it is outside. If worse comes to worst, we could probably walk home," Jake said.

Worst had already come. When they looked out the front entry, the streetlight that was only ten feet away was barely visible. Everything else was obscured from view by an angry, swirling, blowing blanket of snow. Added to that, the door was locked on the inside.

"Great," Jake muttered. "Even if someone comes for us, we can't get out."

"One of the librarians has to have a key."

"They don't know we're here," Jake reminded her.

"Joanna and Ernie probably have keys."

"Joanna thinks we're home. So does Ernie."

"When our folks figure out what's happened, they'll find *somebody*," Addie snapped, annoyed with her cousin's pessimism.

"That could be a while."

Addie finally acknowledged their dilemma and sighed. "They must turn the heat down when they leave," she said. "I'm freezing."

"Me, too," Jake agreed. "Let's go back down-stairs and get our coats."

"Good idea," Addie said. They made their way across the ever-darkening room and ran down the stairs to the lighted basement. Jake accidentally bumped the carton that held the door open. It slid to one side and the door closed quietly behind him.

They found their coats and Addie slipped into hers quickly. Jake followed suit and tucked their book inside his jacket.

"Let's go back upstairs and find the lights," he suggested. "If we turn them all on, someone's bound to see it sooner or later and call the police."

"Okay," Addie agreed. "Should we turn out the lights down here?"

"Yeah," Jake said. "The switch is by the door."

Addie flicked off the lights just as Jake turned the doorknob. But the doorknob wouldn't turn, and Addie's heart nose-dived into her stomach.

Jake rattled the knob and pulled hard on the door, to no avail. Addie flicked on the lights, and the two children stared at one another in disbelief.

Finally Addie spoke. "Well, look at it this way," she said. "There's not much else that can go wrong."

Above them, the telephone rang.

"Guess again," Jake said glumly.

CHAPTER 13

The Treasure

The phone finally stopped ringing.

"Do you think that was one of our parents?" Addie asked her cousin.

Jake shrugged. "Hope it wasn't my dad. Should be interesting to see how he blames me for this."

"What did you talk about last night?" Addie wanted to know.

"He ... apologized," Jake admitted.

Addie didn't say anything for several moments. "He's trying, Jake. Maybe you should meet him halfway."

When Jake didn't answer, Addie tried again. "Gram said Uncle Lee and Grandpa had a hard time getting along, too."

Jake nodded. "You could see it in those pictures in Gram's album. I recognized the look on his face. I know just how he felt, not being one of the group."

He looked surprised at what he'd just said and Addie laughed.

"Maybe you've got more in common than you realize," she said.

"Maybe," he said reluctantly. He got to his feet and changed the subject. "Surely there's an exit in this basement," he said.

There was, but it was locked too. "Do you suppose they keep extra door keys around here?" Addie asked. "If we could find one and get out, I'm sure we could make it down the block to Irlene's house."

"If she's home," Jake answered gloomily. "Face it, Addie, I think we're stuck here for a while. *If* Joanna and Ernie figure out what happened, the first thing they'll do is call Gram's to see if someone else picked us up. Of course, the answer to that is no, so they'll call the library to make sure we're all right. When we don't answer, they'll assume we went somewhere else, or they'll think we tried to walk home."

"So someone will probably start looking for us, but they'll be looking in all the wrong places," Addie concluded.

Jake nodded and rolled his eyes. "My mom's going to freak if she thinks I'm out wandering around in a blizzard."

Addie turned and slid down the wall to the floor. Jake joined her. She closed her eyes and neither of them spoke for several moments.

"Lord," Addie finally murmured, "please help *someone* figure out what's happened. Soon." She paused. "I have to go to the bathroom."

Jake chuckled and Addie poked him. "It's not funny."

"I bet there's a bathroom down here somewhere," he said.

"They probably keep it locked," Addie muttered.

They got to their feet and walked to one end of the basement. They knew which room was storage; they'd seen Ernie go in and out of that door several times. There were two more doors there. One was a furnace room, the other was the utility room where Ernie stored his cleaning cart.

"How about down at that end?" Jake said.

There was only one door on that wall. To Addie's relief, it was a small bathroom—and it was unlocked.

"You start looking for keys to the outside doors," Addie told her cousin.

When she came back to Joanna's desk, Jake had made himself at home. His feet were propped up on an open drawer and he was thumbing through the pages of a typewritten list.

"No keys," he said.

Addie pulled open the top drawer. Jake dropped his feet to the floor and scooted out of her way.

"So don't believe me," he grinned. "Look for yourself."

Addie did just that and spent the next several minutes combing the contents of each drawer, underneath it, and behind it. No keys.

"Satisfied?" Jake asked.

Addie just wrinkled her nose at him. "What are you reading?"

"It's a list of things they've found in the storage rooms," he said. "Listen to some of this stuff. 'Abacus. Adding machine. Andiron. Atlas, 1929—'"

"Andiron?" Addie exclaimed. "In a library?"

"Maybe they had a fireplace at one time," Jake shrugged. "It gets better. 'Barbells. Calculators (4). Canning jars. Christmas tree—'"

Addie interrupted him again. "I don't understand why a library would have that kind of stuff in their storage room."

"This is just a list of 'Objects—Owner/Origin Unknown,'" he read. "The second list is a lot longer. It has the names of books, papers, magazines, that kind of stuff. Library stuff."

Addie took the list from him and studied it. There was another paper stapled to the back, but it was handwritten, not typed. Addie flipped back and forth between the different pages several times.

"Oh, I see," she finally said. "The typewritten lists are from the first two rooms, the rooms they're done with. This list," she showed him the final page, "is everything they've found in the room they're working on now."

Jake nodded. Joanna's handwriting was clear and firm, but the page was difficult to read because she had written notes and names and titles all at different angles with different-colored pens and pencils.

"'Johnson family grave decorations,'" Jake read. He flipped the page around. "'Photo essay, history of Camp Point.' That sounds interesting. 'M. Brockworth Chalmers, small camelback trunk.'"

Jake did a double take, and Addie grabbed the paper from his hands.

"M. Brockworth!" she practically shouted. "That's her! That's Nolda's best friend! Brockworth was her maiden name. Is there anything else about her?"

The two children scoured the page and Jake found her name again at the bottom.

"M. Chalmers, 1925–1945. What's that?" He stopped and pointed. "Look. It says 'Librarians' and there are four more names here. She must have been the librarian here for 20 years."

"And her camelback trunk is in the storage room!"

The two children practically fell over one another in their race to the storage room at the far end of the library. Jake got there first. He reached for the knob and pulled.

Locked.

Addie groaned out loud and Jake rattled the knob and pounded on the door in frustration.

"Okay, okay," Addie said. "Let's just calm down and think. Joanna has her keys, but she must have spares because Ernie has to get in there a lot so—"

"*Ernie!*" Both children shouted the name and bolted for the room two doors down. The utility room was not locked and the cleaning cart was right inside the door. Looped over the top of a bottle of disinfectant was a piece of twine with a key dangling at the end.

"Thank You, Lord!" Addie breathed and grabbed the key. They went back to the storage room and opened the door.

The first room smelled of disinfectant and it was obvious it had been cleaned. Books and papers were stacked neatly on shelves and cartons with large white labels lined the walls. There were two more doors, one to their left and one at the back of the room.

The door to the left opened into a smaller room. It also showed obvious signs of recent organization, although it was a little dustier and the floor had not been washed.

"Think they're getting tired of cleaning this place?" Jake asked with a grin.

"I would be," Addie answered.

They entered the last room and Addie flicked on the light switch next to the door. This room gave them a true picture of the monstrous task Joanna and Ernie had faced. The dust in the air was so thick Addie could feel it in her nose when she breathed. Cobwebs hung from the corners and the tiny window close to the ceiling was so dirty it was almost impossible to see the storm that raged outside.

The light in the ceiling was a single, bare bulb. It cast strange shadows and gave the room a worn-out look. Boxes were stacked, some as high as Addie's head, and books lined every wall. There were piles of newspapers tied up with strings scattered around the floor.

Jake sniffed and rubbed his nose. "This is disgusting," he said.

Addie looked at her cousin. "Jake . . ." she began.

Jake nodded. "I know what you're thinking. But I really don't believe Joanna would care that we're in here. I mean, it's not like we're going to mess up the place," he grinned. "With all the dust I've got up my nose and on my clothes, it'll probably be cleaner when we leave. And we're not going to go through anyone else's stuff, right?"

Addie nodded. "Right. So what's a camelback trunk, anyway?"

"A trunk with a hump on the top," Jake said. "Some have flat tops, some don't. You can't stack anything on top of a camelback trunk, so it should be easy to find."

"They've already found it, remember?" Addie said.

"Oh, yeah. Do you see any piles that look like they've been organized?" he asked.

Addie surveyed the room doubtfully. "Maybe . . . over there," she pointed.

That particular corner held the same stacks of boxes and papers that were everywhere else, but these had been moved away from the wall. Jake and Addie climbed over the papers in the middle of the floor and peered behind two boxes that were so old they were splitting at the corners and the sides sagged.

"Bingo," Jake said softly. He pushed one box to the side. It tore and sagged even more. He waited to make sure nothing was going to fall out, then he pushed the other box to the other side. It remained intact. That gave them enough room to pull out the trunk. Jake took one handle and Addie took the other, but Addie's tore out in her hand.

"Uh-oh," she winced.

"Don't worry about it," Jake said. "This whole thing is ready to fall apart."

Addie managed to get behind the trunk and she pushed while Jake pulled. They drug the cumbersome trunk to the middle of the floor, under the light, to get a better look.

The trunk was in a sad state of disrepair. The leather that once covered the whole thing had fallen off in huge pieces, exposing the wood frame. The name *Brockworth* was still discernible on the front, although the letters *R, C, K,* and *O* were missing. The metal trim had rusted and the latch on one side was completely gone. The latch in the middle was still intact, and it was bolted shut with an old-fashioned, round padlock that seemed very substantial indeed.

"Of course it's locked," Jake sighed.

Addie grinned. She reached inside her coat and unzipped the pocket that held the letter. She pulled it out and unwrapped the key. Jake stared at her, astounded.

"Do you carry that with you everywhere you go?" he asked.

"Of course not," Addie laughed. "But I thought we'd probably be visiting Irlene again and I wanted to show her the key. I thought it might jog her memory."

Jake was still shaking his head in disbelief as Addie inserted the large skeleton key in the lock. It turned easily and with a satisfying click, the lock popped open.

Jake pushed the lid up and the rusty hinges protested with a shriek that rivaled fingernails on a chalkboard. The trunk was filled to overflowing with papers, photo albums, and small boxes of all shapes and sizes. Addie was overwhelmed.

"Where do we start?" she moaned.

Jake made a quick decision. "With the fancy boxes," he said. "Irlene said Nolda was proud of her treasure. She wouldn't store it in a box like this." He picked up a cardboard cigar box and opened it. It was full of handkerchiefs. "See?"

"Okay," Addie said. They began taking out boxes and stacking them carefully next to the trunk. There were several "fancy" ones and they examined each carefully. They were almost to the bottom of the trunk when they found what they were looking for.

A small wooden box, about six inches square, sat on top of a larger photo album. The initials NKE were carved in the top and Addie lifted it out gingerly.

"This is it, Jake," she whispered. "Nolda Kelley Elder."

"Open it," he hissed.

She giggled nervously and pried the top off. Inside was a small velvet pouch. Jake picked it up and whistled.

"Lift this," he said and handed it to Addie.

It was surprisingly heavy. She worked her finger inside the draw bag and opened it up. There were five small, dingy yellow rocks inside and she poured them into Jake's hand. They both stared.

"It's kind of ugly," Addie finally said.

Jake laughed. "It's not refined. Feel how soft it is." He pressed one of the rocks between his thumb and forefinger. Addie did the same and her eyes lit up.

"This is so cool," she breathed.

"What else is there?" Jake asked. He slipped the gold nuggets back in their pouch.

Addie lifted a long silver chain with a silver medallion from the box. The steamship *Crown Jewel* was engraved on one side. On the other was a simple message—*To W. with love. H.*

"That's nice," Addie said softly.

Jake nodded. "What else?"

The only other item in the box was another tintype. Jake picked up it up and frowned. "It's the same picture Gram's got upstairs," he said, disappointed.

"No, it's not," Addie said. "Look at the baby. You can hardly see her. There's a shadow over her face."

"A shadow?" Jake picked up Addie's letter and skimmed through it. "'. . . she will grow up not in the shadow of great men, but following in their footsteps,'" he read from the letter. "Whose shadow is it?"

Addie sucked in her breath so sharply she almost choked.

"What?" Jake asked. He followed her gaze and his mouth dropped open.

In the crowd of people to the left of Winnie and the baby, the profile of a tall, thin man was evident. His features were gaunt, his beard somewhat scraggly. The black top hat that was his trademark cast a shadow across the picture and across the face of Addie Haile.

"There wasn't a lion in the picture," Addie McCormick whispered. "It was *Lincoln* in the picture!"

EPILOGUE

"My True Legacy"

The gold lay on the floor forgotten. Addie couldn't take her eyes off the profile of Abraham Lincoln.

"What a great legacy," Jake finally managed to say. Addie could only nod.

"What will you do with it?" he asked.

Addie hadn't even thought about it, but she knew instantly what she would do. "Frame it and hang it on Gram's wall."

Jake smiled. "Gram's going to freak," he murmured.

Addie giggled and suddenly the two of them were sitting on the floor, laughing until their sides hurt. That was how Joanna, Addie's father, and Uncle Lee found them.

"Yep, I knew it. They've been paralyzed with fear." Uncle Lee's booming voice was so unexpected Addie's laughter scaled up to a high-pitched squeal. Then both children were on their feet, chattering with excitement.

"We're sorry, Joanna—"

"We just had to get in here! We found—"

"The treasure's been here all the time—"

"Whoa! Slow down," Addie's father laughed. "One at a time. Start at the beginning." He reached out and pulled his daughter close, hugging her tightly.

Addie took a deep, shaky breath. "I'm sorry, Dad. I hope you weren't too worried. We called, but we didn't know if you heard us or not."

Her father nodded. "We did. You sounded like you were calling from Siberia, but we heard you."

"Jake thought you would," Addie told them.

Uncle Lee gave Jake's shoulder a squeeze. "I figured Jake would keep his head," he said. Jake gave him a surprised glance and his dad smiled ruefully. "You've got a lot more sense than I give you credit for sometimes, son."

Jake studied his shoes, but there was a smile on his lips and Addie could tell he was pleased.

"What's this about your treasure?" Joanna broke the awkward silence.

"We were looking through your desk to see if we could find a key to the door. We didn't, but we saw the paper that you typed up."

Joanna looked puzzled.

"The list of things in the storage rooms," Jake said and the woman nodded.

"The back page had Mary Brockworth's name on it. That's the woman who last had the family treasure. My great-great-great-grandmother gave it to her for safekeeping," Addie explained to Joanna.

"When we saw there was a trunk that belonged to her in the storage room, we had to get in here. So we found the key—and the treasure!"

"Your treasure was here?" Joanna was incredulous. "In the library? In *my* storage room?" She began to laugh. "That's wonderful!"

"Addie?" Her father's voice was urgent. "You found the gold?"

Addie stooped and picked up the wooden box and its contents. She showed her father the small velvet pouch, and he and Uncle Lee examined the nuggets carefully.

"Here's the necklace," Addie held up the medallion. "And here's the real treasure," she said.

Her father took the tintype and frowned. "It looks like the same picture you found at Gram's."

Addie pointed to the baby's face. "See the shadow?"

Her father nodded. "Yeah . . ." He stopped and a grin split his face. "Honest Abe!"

"What?" Uncle Lee took the tintype. He shook his head and began to laugh. "We had Gram's magnifying glass out this afternoon, looking at the words on the other picture. The best we could make out, it said, 'Lion ruined the first picture.'"

"*Lincoln* ruined the first picture," Addie and Jake chorused, and Joanna gasped. Uncle Lee handed her the picture and she took it, almost reverently.

"What a treasure," she finally said.

"Let's get home and show the family what you've got," Uncle Lee said. "Your mother was frantic when she thought you'd left the library," he told Jake. "We'll call first."

The ride home was slow. The wind had died down but it was still snowing hard. They dropped Joanna off at her apartment a few blocks away.

"Thanks for everything," Addie said. "You've really been great."

"Yeah, thanks," Jake echoed.

"If you're free—and the weather permits, of course—we'd love to have you at my mother's birthday party tomorrow," John McCormick said. "I'm sure everyone would like to hear about your part in all of this."

"Thanks," Joanna said. "I'll try to make it. Bye, kids."

When they finally arrived home, and everyone was settled in the kitchen with hot chocolate, Addie and Jake retold their story, culminating in the discovery of the picture of Abe Lincoln.

Gram was speechless when Addie handed her the tintype. Tears filled her eyes and she couldn't speak for several moments. Finally she said, "Addie and Jake, I can't begin to tell you how grateful I am that you stuck with this. You've written a whole new chapter in our family's history."

She tried to hand the picture back to Addie, but the young girl refused. "I want you to have it, Gram. Frame it and hang it on your wall."

"Sweetheart, it's your legacy—"

But Addie shook her head. "I learned a lot about my true legacy," she said. "You gave it to me a long time ago, when you raised my dad to be a Christian," Addie said. "All my grandmothers passed on their faith. I'm grateful to have that. This is a wonderful picture, but it belongs to the whole family," she said. "And it belongs here."

There were murmurs of consent and Gram smiled. "I'll be happy to hang it here for as long as you like," she said.

Then she picked up the medallion. "The *Crown Jewel*," Gram said. "I remember the name now. And of course I remember Mary Chalmers. I never knew her maiden name was Brockworth." She sighed. "I'm positive I wrote all that down. I still remember the paper I used. It was some of Granny Nolda's stationery. Very pretty paper, pale blue with gold edges."

Abe began to dig in his pockets and soon his tiny hands pulled out several pieces of crumpled paper, pale blue with gold trim.

"Like this?" he asked. "I found these behind the stairs."

"I bet they slipped back there when Addie fell that first night," Uncle Denny said.

Addie picked one up and read the words. "'*M. Chalmers kept all my things from the fire. NKE*'"

Jake read another. "'*Winifred Haile's husband went down with the Crown Jewel. NKE*'"

They turned in unison to stare at their young cousin.

Abe gave them a bright smile. "I love pretty paper," he said.

About the Author

Leanne Lucas grew up reading mysteries by a creek near her childhood home in central Illinois. Secret visits to a nearby abandoned house later provided the inspiration for many of Addie's adventures. Leanne enjoys naming her characters after friends and family—Addie was named for a woman she worked with at the University of Illinois.

Leanne and her husband, David, own their own business and homeschool their son, Joshua. They reside in Homer, Illinois, where they share their home with Josh's grandma, four hermit crabs, and a cat named Star.

Don't Miss Any
Addie McCormick Adventures!
by Leanne Lucas

The Action Never Stops in
The Crista Chronicles
by Mark Littleton

Secrets of Moonlight Mountain

When an unexpected blizzard traps Crista on Moonlight Mountain with a young couple in need of a doctor, Crista must brave the storm and the dark to get her physician father. Will she make it in time?

Winter Thunder

A sudden change in Crista's new friend, Jeff, and the odd circumstances surrounding Mrs. Oldham's broken windows all point to Jeff as the culprit in the recent cabin break-ins. What is Jeff trying to hide? Will Crista be able to prove his innocence?

Robbers on Rock Road

When the clues fall into place regarding the true identity of the cabin-wreckers, Crista and her friends find themselves facing terrible danger! Can they stop the robbers on Rock Road before someone gets hurt?

Escape of the Grizzly

A grizzly is on the loose on Moonlight Mountain! Who will find the bear first—the sheriff's posse or the circus workers? Crista knows there isn't much time... the bear has to be found quickly. But where, and how? Doing some fast thinking, Crista comes up with a plan...

Find Adventure and Excitement in
The Maggie Series
by Eric Wiggin

———

Maggie: Life at The Elms

Maggie's father died at the Battle of Gettysburg, and the man her mother is going to marry has a son who Maggie just can't stand! She asks for permission to live with her grandpa in the deep woods of northern Maine—at his special home, The Elms.

Little does Maggie know how much her life is about to change—all because of an overfriendly hound dog, a rude, sharp-tongued girl at a logging camp, clever kitchen thieves in the night, and surprising lessons about friendship and forgiveness.

Maggie's Homecoming

After two years in the deep woods with Grandpa, Maggie is eager to return home. She and her step-brother, Jack, must learn to get along—and to everyone's amazement, they do!

Before she has a chance to settle in to her new home, Maggie is caught in another adventure. One Saturday she and Jack decide to explore a long-abandoned farmhouse around the mountainside—only to find out the place isn't abandoned after all . . .